Days To
Remember

Patsy Collins

The author can be found at
www.patsycollins.uk

ISBN: 978-1-914339-46-2

Contents

1. Family Reunion

"What's this then?" I asked Clover as I pulled the card from the envelope.

Dear Bev, You're invited to a family reunion at the bandstand in Victoria Park, Little Mallow, at 2 pm on Saturday 19th November.

p.s. It's a great dog walking spot!

Clover wagged her stubby tail and looked hopefully at her lead. She can't read, obviously – that's her response to pretty much everything. She can't really answer my questions either, at least not in any detail, but she understands me.

The invitation wasn't signed which seemed peculiar. The timing made sense – the run up to Christmas makes people wish they had others to be with and think of those they previously shared the festival with. At least, that's true in my case. But why would a family need to reunite? That seemed an odd concept. If you had family didn't you stick together, keep in touch?

I'd thought that was the point – unconditional love, forgive and forget. I'd attempted to push my various foster carers into proving they were more loving, caring and supportive than my idealised version of a real family. Of course that hadn't gone well and, disillusioned, I'd returned to the children's home. I'd been wrong. You can build a family without blood ties, but it takes time and effort on both sides.

It was getting Clover which made me understand that how someone comes into your life doesn't affect how much you love them.

"And I do love you, girl," I said, scratching between her floppy brown ears.

Clover isn't a person, but she has as much personality as any human. To be frank she's more important to me than any actual person, but then I don't have many people in my life. Nobody special. That's my fault, I know that now.

It wasn't my fault I was born to people unwilling to accept the responsibilities of parenthood. It wasn't really my fault that as a child I found that difficult to cope with – although I could have made life easier for those who tried to help me. It's definitely my fault that since becoming an adult I've pushed people away before they have the chance to reject me.

"Oh, Clover, when will I ever learn?"

She tilted her head to one side, inviting me to explain.

"Martin, from the shelter where I adopted you? I could tell he was nice and kind, not just from his job, but the way dogs in his care responded to him, but I wasn't nice and kind back."

To start with it had been OK. I'd volunteered for a few hours each week, walking dogs and cleaning their pens. I wanted to prove to myself that I didn't just like the idea of having a cute ball of fluff to give me an enthusiastic welcome when I came home, but was prepared for the realities of owning one.

Martin had been the one to show me what to do when I started. Later he'd clearly welcomed my regular arrivals, usually arranged things so we worked together, and I'd thought we were becoming friends. Thought I'd let that happen. Occasionally I fantasised about becoming more than friends. Partly with that in mind I'd decided to continue volunteering after I got a dog of my own. I didn't tell him any of that of course, just asked for the forms I needed to start the process of adopting a puppy. That last word was a slip of the tongue as I'd been willing to take on an adult dog. When I tried to correct that, say I knew the benefits to owning older dogs, I suppose it came out wrong – gave the impression I didn't want to bother with all the training.

"Bev, are you sure?" he asked. "If you keep volunteering here then you can walk a dog whenever you like… "

I cut him off, by yelling, "Of course I'm sure! I know what it's like to be abandoned and won't do that to the poor creature."

"OK, right. I'll get you those forms."

Someone better at reading other people's emotions, someone like Clover, might have wondered if one of the things I'd prevented him from saying was that he'd like me to keep volunteering and not just because I was useful. They might have guessed his reaction, once it seemed I wasn't going to keep coming back, was disappointment. But me being me I took it as proof I shouldn't have hoped for any kind of relationship with him and did nothing to try to repair our friendship. I didn't give him a chance to try either, in case he didn't grasp the opportunity.

When I arrived for my volunteer stints I tried to avoid him. As that proved impossible, I was polite but cool. He always said hello, asked if I was well, mentioned the tasks to be done.

My reply was always, "I'm fine. Can I work with Carly today?" Or John, or Ishana, or alone.

A simple, "Can I give you a hand?" when he said what he'd be doing might have been enough. Almost certainly would have been, but I didn't take the tiny risk that friendly, polite Martin might rebuff me so harshly it would put a dent in my defensive barrier.

"Bev, you know there has to be a home visit before you can be approved to adopt?" he asked one day.

"Absolutely," I said brightly. "I'm looking forward to proving I can provide a good home. My flat is small, but the landlady is happy for me to use the garden and has even promised to let my dog out for a while each day. I work close by so can come home and do the same every lunchtime, so she wouldn't be shut in alone all day."

"That sounds perfect."

I almost said, "Come and see," but assumed he'd be doing that as part of his job. What I did do was pop down the bakery on the morning arranged for the visit and buy a few cookies and doughnuts. That, I thought, was a friendly thing to do, might prolong the visit and make it more of a social situation. I was right. Carly, Martin's colleague, was very happy to accept some refreshments and stayed chatting for quite a while.

"Is everything OK then?" I asked. "You'll let me have a dog?" I'd requested a small female of gentle temperament. The size of my flat meant a large or boisterous breed wouldn't be ideal, and my landlady said she'd prefer one which didn't cock his leg on her hydrangeas.

"The next suitable one is yours," Carly promised.

In case that happened sooner rather than later I warned my boss I'd be wanting time off to help my new pet settle in. She agreed and brought forward a training course I was due to go on, so I needn't worry about kennels.

I was away when Carly rang to say she had a puppy which might suit me. "She's six months old, house trained and not too bad on a lead, but hasn't been taught anything beyond that. The previous owners' dog had puppies They wanted to keep them all but simply couldn't cope. Thankfully they realised before things reached a crisis."

4

"She sounds perfect."

"When can you come and take a look?"

After I explained about the course, Carly agreed to keep the pup until my return in three days' time.

One look at Clover was all it took for me to fall in love.

"We'll all miss you at the shelter," Carly said, once the formalities were completed.

Thankfully I realised that wasn't a hint I was no longer welcome. She knew that when I first volunteered it was only to be until I had a dog of my own. Her words meant she really would miss me. And she had said 'all'.

"You have my number and know the hours I work. If you're ever stuck for someone to come in outside those times, give me a call."

"Really? That would be fantastic!"

A sympathetic licking of my fingers made me see things in a slightly more positive light. "You're right, Clover, I have learned my lesson."

I'd missed my chance, my possible chance anyway, of forming a deeper and long-lasting relationship with Martin, but I was determined not to repeat that mistake.

I returned my attention to the invitation I'd received. Refusing a kindly meant invitation might be a mistake. Most likely me receiving it was also a mistake, but I couldn't be sure. Some of my foster parents would have sent birthday and Christmas cards if I'd kept in touch. They might even have invited me to a wedding or other party, but I hadn't given any of them my new address or any reason to think I ever gave them a kind thought. I promised myself I'd try to put that right. A pretty card with a few words of thanks for giving me a safe home and saying I was doing OK might be appreciated and if I didn't invite a response I needn't feel rejected if none were forthcoming.

It did cross my mind for a moment that my birth family were trying to make contact. It seemed unlikely. Very unlikely. My social worker had explained all the procedures and stuff and none of it involved giving my address out so someone could send me an anonymous invitation. There was only one way I could learn who'd sent it.

"Shall we go?" I asked Clover. The meeting was to be in a public place, in daylight, so I was sure it would be safe. And the p.s. made it clear I could take Clover, who I'd be walking then anyway.

Clover must have picked up from my tone of voice that an outing of some kind was on offer, so resumed her tail wagging and hopeful looks towards her lead.

"OK then, that's settled." I wouldn't be going as a guest, I was almost certain I wasn't the intended recipient of the invitation, I just wanted to take a look and satisfy my curiosity.

On the 19th I was unable to spot a family group waiting to be joined by others. I was sure they'd stand out if they were there. It was a beautifully bright day and mild for November, but breezy so nobody would linger without reason.

I did recognise a lady walking her own dog. We'd exchanged a few words now and then, on account of our dogs being the same breed and age. When I say breed, I mean about the same size and shape and a similar colour. They're not pedigree or anything.

"Hello!" I called and headed in the lady's direction. In part that was so I could hang around and look for the reuniting family without seeming a weirdo. Also it was because the lady seemed nice when we'd spoken before and as though the short conversations were welcome. Although she was about three decades older than me, I thought maybe we could become friends.

We walked as we talked. Soon I discovered her name was Yvonne – previously only Clover and Toffee had been introduced. I learned she was as nice as the initial impression suggested, a widow and had got Toffee so she wasn't too lonely.

"It's nice to have someone to talk to, even if they do pretend to think every other comment is an invitation to go for a W.A.L.K. or an offer of a T.R.E.A.T. isn't it?"

I completely agreed, and grasped the opportunity offered to me. "Maybe we could W.A.L.K. them together sometimes? Clover is a brilliant listener, but not very chatty."

"Oh, that would be nice! When would be convenient for you?"

We decided on about the same time, same place as we'd met that day. We exchanged phone numbers and promises there was no pressure if either of us was busy or didn't feel like it.

"Excuse me, am I in the right place?" asked a man of around my own age. "The invitation said the bandstand, but there's nobody there."

"We were," Yvonne said. "But it was cold standing still."

"You're here for the family reunion too?" I asked them both. Then I think we all noticed each others' dogs at the same time. His looked even more like Clover than Yvonne's Toffee did.

As Bill introduced himself and Jasper, an older couple, with another matching dog, joined us.

"We're Ted and May Jackson," the man said. "And this is Oscar."

"This reunion thing is making sense now," Yvonne said. "It's for our dogs. They must be from the same litter, don't you think?"

We agreed they must. We established that Carly had carried out the shelter's home visit for all of us. It seemed entirely possible she'd sent the invitations. Allowing the litter to meet up was a lovely idea and surely good for the dogs and their owners. Her method of arranging it was a bit peculiar, but I didn't know her well. Maybe she liked to act in unconventional ways.

"Shall we walk across to the bandstand?" May Jackson suggested. "It's not much warmer in there, but it does give a bit of shelter from the wind and we put a bag of treats in there."

Whether it was the word 'treats' or 'walk' which set her off I don't know, but Toffee yapped excitedly and spun round in circles. Clover, Jasper and Oscar were soon joining in.

"Luckily there's something for everyone," May said.

As we walked, Bill remarked that anyone seeing us might think we were as much a family as our dogs. "Ted and May could be mine and Bev's parents."

"Grandparents more like!" May said.

"You know, I do feel a kind of connection with you all. Especially Bev as I've met her before and we're going to meet to W.A.L.K. our dogs together. That's going to be such a treat. Whoops!" That last was because Toffee had gone into another mini frenzy, which set Jasper off and the pair of them almost knocked Bill off his feet.

"Is it too cheeky to ask if I can join you sometimes? I can give Jasper plenty of wal… umm W.A.L.K.S. but it's not the same as scampering around like this, and they're having a lot of fun."

"I don't mind a bit of cheek," Yvonne said. "How about you, Bev?"

"I think it would be lovely for the dogs to all get together." Bill seemed pleasant and I guessed he was thinking a group walk would be a nice change, but I was sure Yvonne was reading more into his request than he meant.

"Us too?" May asked. "Like Bill here we take Oscar out regularly, but our pace is sedate. Seeing them playing together like this makes me realise he'd benefit from more energetic exercise."

I explained the arrangement Yvonne and I had made and we all exchanged numbers. Despite the chill in the air I felt a warm glow. In truth I hardly knew these people, yet I had no doubt that if I ever felt low or in need of company I could call any of them and say, 'Do you fancy a walk?' And even if they didn't want to go out they wouldn't mind that I'd asked and would probably chat for a bit. I'd be the same if one of them phoned me. That's how I think of family. Someone you can call for no reason at all and who can contact you without explanation or making you wonder what they want.

As Ted distributed the kind of chews Clover and her siblings adore and are supposedly good for their teeth, May did an excellent impression of a doting Gran. She supplied us all with wedges of Victoria sandwich cake, "Because we're in Victoria Park," and beakers of hot chocolate, "Because it's November and everyone likes chocolate."

None of us could fault her logic.

"You're extremely well prepared," Yvonne remarked.

"An unbreakable habit. We used to be emergency foster carers," Ted said.

I knew they'd not fostered me as all the families I'd stayed with were younger, but still felt there was something I should say. "Thank you, both of you. I grew up in foster care, so owe a lot to people like you." I explained my regret about not staying in touch and about the notes I intended to send. I've never opened up quite like that before, but even with Yvonne and Bill listening in I didn't feel awkward.

"That's a lovely idea, Bev," May said. "It means a great deal to us when we hear from any of our kids. We fostered for over forty years and although it was sensible to stop while we're still reasonably fit, I do miss being the centre of a family and I know Ted feels the same."

"So go on, adopt Bev and I as part time grandkids!" Bill said.

"No, no," Yvonne said. "Oh, sorry, I don't mean about forming an unofficial family. That's a wonderful idea and I hope I can be a cousin or something. What I mean is that Ted and May didn't bring a bar of chocolate big enough to share and an extra dog T.R.E.A.T. You brought enough of everything for us all, as though you knew who would be here and that we'd have our dogs."

"Tell them, Ted."

"We did know. Martin discussed the idea with us before sending the invitations."

"Martin!" My voice was probably quite high and loud. "Is Martin coming here?"

Ted waved his mobile phone. "He is if you'd like him to."

"I'm sure none of will object to that," Yvonne said.

"You're right, Cousin Yvonne, nobody will object, but that's not the issue. Martin will be here like a shot, but only if that's what our Bev really wants."

"I do," I confirmed. "I want that very much."

As Ted made the call, Bill pretended to punch me on the arm. "Did you hear that, Aunty Yvonne? My little sis is in L.O.V.E.."

Yvonne blushed and I'm pretty sure I did too. She recovered more quickly. "Which am I, cousin or aunt?"

"Both?" Bill suggested. "I'm no good at the maths, but can't you be Ted and May's cousin and aunt to me and Bev?"

"I think that works," Ted said. "And me and May are Granny and Gramps."

"And Martin? Will he be part of this family?" Yvonne asked.

"That's up to him and Bev, but I have him down as Bill's future brother-in-law."

"Oh, I do love a wedding! I'm going to start looking at hats!" May said.

"Who's getting married?" asked Martin, as he stepped up into the bandstand.

Gramps ignored the question and mentioned our weekly walks. As he managed to get the words 'walk' and 'treat' in at least three times everyone was distracted and the conversation moved on. Maybe one day Martin and I will resume it on our own. I very much hope so, but whatever happens, Clover and I have many family reunions to look forward to.

2. Christmas Comes Early

The cartoon ended and was replaced with an advert about a winter wonderland park celebrating the magic of Christmas, due to open early December. Anne wondered how soon after that the complaints would start. Those events always seemed to be a disaster. Fake snow failing to cover the mud, scenery toppling over in the wind and mix ups with tickets were almost a certainty. Just as likely was Santa slurring his words and the elves all smelling of tobacco and barely bothering to smile as the few dispirited members of the public straggled past. She'd give anything to be able to take her daughter though. For Hannah to be strong enough to go out in the cold and stand to stroke the one mangy looking reindeer and a few random animals to represent the nativity.

If they were lucky, Hannah would be propped up in a hospital bed watching the presents she'd never get to play with being unwrapped for her. If they were unlucky, they'd be no need to spend Christmas day in the hospital.

"Will it be Christmas soon, Mum?"

"A few months yet, love."

"I wish it would hurry up! I need some Christmas magic!"

What Hannah needed was a miracle. There was research into her condition going on, new drugs being tested, so it was just possible, Anne reminded herself. She must stay positive.

Jonathan returned to the ward with a pack of Hannah's favourite crisps.

"Thank you, Daddy." She managed to eat two and washed them down with a sip of milk. They all watched the next cartoon together without Hannah once complaining she felt nauseous; maybe she really was improving.

The winter wonderland didn't feature during the next set of adverts, but there was one for an expensive electronic game.

"Christmas gets earlier every year!" Jonathan said.

"Then it won't be a really long time?" Hannah asked.

"Here before you know it, love." Jonathan said. He never could deny her much, even before she was sick. Now there wasn't anything he'd say no to. He'd gone to huge trouble for her birthday party. It had been worth the effort just to see her so happy and take a few more pictures to treasure, but there was an unexpected bonus. Hannah had eaten some of the cake and jelly. Not much, not nearly enough, but some. Somehow her brain had convinced her stomach that party foods were different and could be retained.

After they'd kissed Hannah goodnight and left the hospital, Anne said, "Let's bring Christmas forward."

"We can't do that."

"Why not? Hannah loves Christmas and at the moment she's well enough to enjoy some of it. No one really knows what day it's supposed to be anyway. Maybe the day we pick will be the right one?"

"I understand why you want to, but can we really do it?"

It seemed they could. Family, friends and neighbours all agreed to join in. After much coaxing and agreeing to conditions, the hospital agreed that Hannah could spend a few days at home after her next round of chemotherapy. While other people prepared for Hallowe'en and bonfire night, Anne and Jonathan encouraged their daughter to look forward to a special Christmas. They brought in mince pies, clementines, marzipan and every edible Christmassy treat they could think of. Hannah nibbled a little of everything and spoke so enthusiastically about going home for Christmas that Anne knew they were doing the right thing.

Hannah said she didn't want presents. "I have enough toys. Give the money to the people who are looking for the way to make me better." Her parents cried at that proof their little girl understood the seriousness of her situation.

Hannah dozed in the car on the way home. When they were almost there Jonathan sent a text to their neighbours, then woke Hannah.

"Look at the lights, love."

Anne drove round in circles so Hannah could see the lights several neighbours had strung outside their houses just for her, and it would seem like the whole town was lit up. After a nap Hannah supervised the decorating of the tree and looked at all the cards.

The following day she helped fit lids onto the mince pies and joined in a few words when a group of carol singers called. The local Girl Guides had been happy to provide the out of season entertainment when they heard how much it would mean to a sick little girl. Hannah loved it all. She ate too. Not like a healthy child, but she consumed what for Hannah was an enormous amount.

On Hannah's early Christmas Eve she said she wanted to stay up until midnight so she'd know the moment it really was Christmas Day.

"All right, but you must get into bed." Her parents persuaded her into thick pyjamas, woolly hat and socks and wrapped the far too big dressing gown around her, then read magical Christmas stories.

There was a sound like sleigh bells. Jonathan looked out of the window.

"It must be Christmas. Santa's here!"

He lifted his daughter, quilt and all and carried her downstairs. The man who was to supply the animals for the winter wonderland had brought a reindeer for her to stroke. He was on the large side for an elf, but dressed appropriately.

Hannah stroked the gentle animal, then leaned forward and whispered something into its ear. The reindeer raised and lowered its antlered head as though saying yes.

"Everything is going to be all right now," Hannah said. "I've made a Christmas wish."

On Christmas Day, or November twelfth, depending on whether or not you were part of the Webster household, the phone rang as they were eating Christmas pudding. It was Hannah's consultant to say that unexpectedly there was space on a drug trial.

"There's no guarantee, you know that, but there have been encouraging results from some patients in an earlier trial. Some showed real improvements even before the six weeks were up. We'd like to start as soon as possible. Ideally I'd like her to come back in today so we can get things rolling."

After a quick scramble, Hannah, her parents, and Christmas cake for her friends on the ward, were on their way back to hospital.

"I told you everything will be OK now," Hannah said. "The new medicine is my Christmas miracle and when I've had it all, I will get better." Her voice was strong enough for Anne, who was driving, to hear clearly.

"That's right, love," Jonathan said. He kissed the top of her head.

Anne didn't blame Jonathan for reassuring their daughter, but wasn't quite so optimistic herself. At least she wasn't until she stopped at some lights. Jonathan passed her his diary.

"I've marked out the six weeks. Look when they're up." He'd circled the twenty-fifth of December.

"That new winter wonderland park is staying open until twelfth night. I'm going to book us some tickets as soon as we get home." Shoddy workmanship and bored staff or not, Anne was willing to bet all they'd see would be the magic of Christmas.

3. Something Special

As her gorgeous boyfriend hugged Bella, something small and hard knocked against her ribs. It wasn't painful exactly, but it felt wrong. Joe's hugs were always enthusiastic, but she'd never before felt at risk of gaining a bruise. Of course it was just something in his jacket pocket. Perhaps even something he'd forgotten about, although he wasn't a forgetful person.

"So, where are we going?" she asked. He'd told her it was a surprise and to dress up nice.

"Don't I always?" she'd teased.

"You always look beautiful, but you know what I mean."

Bella had known. She and Joe understood each other. They always had. They weren't telepathic or anything weird, despite what friends claimed, but they knew how the other's mind worked. She could easily guess where he was taking her for their date.

"You're taking me to L'Escargot?" she asked, sure she knew the answer.

"One day I might actually manage to surprise you," he said with a grin.

Bella hoped not. She was perfectly happy with everything exactly as it was. She adored L'Escargot. That wasn't the restaurant's real name. Bella and Joe had watched as the former burger bar was refurbished. It was the year they'd turned eighteen so it felt as though it was growing up in parallel with them. The sign was the flag of France with 'Claire's Café' painted on in gold letters. That hadn't seemed French enough, so they'd come up with their own alternative and always referred to it as L'Escargot, even before they'd ever eaten there.

Other than its name, Bella thoroughly approved of everything about the restaurant. The look of the place, the accents of the staff, the atmosphere, the food, but most of all their shared memories of eating there. They'd celebrated together at L'Escargot when they graduated. Joe had taken her there for her twenty-first birthday and every other time he wanted to give her a special treat. It was a special treat kind of place, not somewhere you went just because you were hungry. So why was Joe taking her there tonight? What was so special about tonight?

It wasn't any kind of anniversary, she was sure of that. They'd met in September when they both started junior school. By the October they'd made a solemn vow to be best friends forever. It was March, ten years later, when they'd first started dating. Bella remembered that because it had taken the entire summer for her to say yes. That wasn't because she didn't want to, just that she was worried it might stop them being best friends. She needn't have worried. She should try not to worry now.

L'Escargot's Maitre d' greeted them warmly and took Bella's coat. Joe opted to keep his jacket with him, which was unusual. As they studied the menu and ordered, he seemed nervous. Just a little. Only someone who knew him as well as Bella would have guessed.

The wine he chose wasn't champagne, but her favourite rich, mellow red. She'd been right then; this wasn't a big celebration.

Bella didn't feel Joe was about to break bad news. L'Escargot wasn't the place for that and besides, his nervousness was more like anticipation than dread.

"To us," Joe said as he raised his glass.

"To us," Bella repeated his toast, tapped her glass to his and took a sip.

"I've been shopping." Joe reached into his jacket, produced a small velvet box, then slipped it back in almost immediately and began talking about the features of his new phone.

Bella barely listened. She had no doubt the box contained a diamond ring and that Joe planned to propose. How could she stop him? It wouldn't be easy, but she had to do it. Saying no, here at L'Escargot, in front of the other diners and the staff would be awful. She couldn't accept either. Marriage would change everything.

It wasn't that she didn't love Joe. She did and had known it even when he'd asked her out that first time. But they'd been friends for so long by then it felt almost wrong to change their relationship. A risk, yes, but not just that. It was like the time her maths teacher, Mrs Jackson, had moved next door to the home Bella shared with her parents. Teachers, Bella had felt, should only be encountered at school. Outside of it they were no longer just teachers and had to be considered in a whole new light.

Eventually Bella had agreed to a date with Joe. She'd told him when they were sitting under the ancient willow overlooking the river. It felt right as that's where they'd made their friendship vow. Later it was the first place they kissed. The memory gave Bella an idea.

"I was thinking about special places," she said when Joe lapsed into silence.

"This is one for us, isn't it?" he said.

"Yes, but… "

"You're right. It's not *the* place."

Bella relaxed. He wasn't going to propose over dinner.

"Are you OK?" Joe asked. "You seem distracted."

"Sorry. My mind is wandering a bit. Do you remember when Mrs Jackson moved next door to me?"

"You hated the idea."

"Not hated, but it took me a while to get used to it."

Actually not that long. It was autumn when she moved in and she'd given Bella and other neighbourhood kids a pound to sweep leaves from her lawn. She'd decorated her house at hallowe'en and given out home made cookies as well as shop bought treats. When, years later, Bella moved into a tiny apartment of her own, Mrs Jackson had been one of the people she'd invited to her housewarming.

Over the delicious meal at L'Escargot, Bella and Joe discussed their shared past and Joe hinted at a future together. A future in which they'd be just as happy as they were right then.

As they left the restaurant he took her hand. "It's a lovely night. Shall we walk up to our tree and see how the river looks in the moonlight?"

He wanted to take a moonlit stroll to their special place, carrying a diamond ring in his pocket... Bella knew what that meant. And now that she'd had time to think about it, she knew how to respond.

"Yes, Joe. Yes."

4. Lost

Caitlin looked as forlorn as Moira felt. "I'm sorry, Mum."

"What on earth for?" Moira asked. She abandoned the unpacking and sank onto the bed in her daughter's tiny student flat. "I'm so proud of you getting into university." It was true, Moira often thought her greatest achievement was producing Caitlin and helping her grow into the wonderful young woman she was.

"Yes, but abandoning you now that Dad…"

Doug hadn't abandoned her exactly. Moira kicked him out when she'd found out about his affair. Or rather his latest affair.

"Don't be silly, love. It's probably good you're away. I'll be able to make a nice fresh start with no one but myself to please."

Moira would have to work hard to make that true, but at least she wouldn't have to risk losing her faith in Caitlin too. The girl would still see her father, of course, but Moira need know nothing about it. Goodness knows, Doug was expert at keeping his visits to young women a secret. She wouldn't think about that now. Her task was to get Caitlin settled.

"I've got something for you."

"Thanks, Mum." As was her habit, Caitlin gently squeezed the gift and guessed what was under the wrapping paper. "It can't be."

Moira grinned at the puzzled expression on her daughter's face as she pulled the stuffed panda free. It was exactly like the one Moira had made her when she'd been a baby. Caitlin had carried it with her everywhere until, in her early teens, the toy disintegrated.

"But, I don't understand."

"I made you a new one," Moira said as though it had been easy. Actually making it had been fairly easy; accepting the pattern from her former friend was the difficult part.

"You'd lost the pattern. You told me so."

"I thought I had, but I'd lent it to Sue and she forgot to give it back." Moira gave a wry smile. She'd only known Sue a few months then. They'd met at antenatal classes, and already Sue had let her down. Probably Doug had too, but Moira hadn't seen the signs and blindly trusted them both.

Sue had arrived at Moira's home a few weeks ago with the pattern. She'd walked straight into the garden as though she still expected to be welcome. "I was looking through the loft and I found this. I remembered how much Caitlin loved that panda."

No use cutting off her nose to spite her face, so Moira accepted the pattern, though not as a peace offering. She'd gone inside, shutting the kitchen door on Sue.

"Thanks, Mum. I love him already," Caitlin said recalling Moira to the present – and the gift.

They chatted for a while until Caitlin said, "You'll have to get going soon if you want to get out the city in daylight."

"All right, I can take a hint!" She winked to show she'd taken no offence.

On the way up she'd had Caitlin beside her, reassuring Moira she recognised the route from the time Doug had driven them up before.

Moira retraced her outward journey until the one-way system made that impossible. She recognised a strangely shaped bush. Doug had turned left just after that, she remembered.

After she'd made the turn she remembered something else; they hadn't gone straight home. The three of them had gone for a pizza. Moira knew she didn't want to go back there. She took the next turning and was soon hopelessly lost. She stopped to study the map. A tear dripped onto the page. What was the point of even trying? There was nothing for her to get home to.

Her husband had gone. Twenty years of marriage and almost every one of them a lie. She'd believed him when he said he'd love, honour and cherish. She believed him when he said he was working late or had business trips away. She'd believed Sue as well when, in her capacity as his secretary, she'd occasionally passed on similar messages.

Moira and Sue had trusted each other with their children, taking turns to nurse them through mumps and chicken pox. They'd been there for each other through every parental worry. Moira had thought Sue would be there through her marital worries too.

Sue hadn't been shocked or reassuring when Moira found a receipt for lingerie in Doug's jacket. She'd just nodded sadly. "Moira, I'm so sorry."

Sorry? That's what Doug had said. It wasn't good enough after twenty years of marriage and it wasn't good enough after nineteen years of what Moira had thought was friendship.

What should she do now? What could she do? She couldn't even trust herself to find her own way home. She'd better ask for directions. Moira stopped, opened the window and leant out.

"Excuse me, can you tell me how to reach the dual carriageway?"

The other woman pointed in the direction Moira was headed, then frowned. "Walking, it's right at the pink house down there but I think it's one-way. Sorry."

"Well, thanks anyway," Moira said.

As the woman had thought, Moira wasn't permitted to enter the road by the pink house. At least she hadn't given misleading information.

Was the same true of Sue? Now Moira thought back, Sue never told an outright lie. Her messages where always along the lines of, "I've been asked to tell you…" She may have guessed what Doug was up to, but with loyalties torn between her friend and boss maybe it wasn't surprising she'd not dug too deep.

Moira's marriage was over and so was Caitlin's childhood, they couldn't be brought back. Perhaps though, just like with the toy panda, Moira could make a new friendship with Sue? After seeking further directions, Moira drove not to her own home, but to Sue's. Outside, she reflected that Sue too was on her own. She'd never had a husband to lose and her son Tom had gone to university in America, so she'd hardly ever see him. Poor woman would need a friend just as much as Moira did. She rang the doorbell and waited on the step.

Sue looked as forlorn as Moira felt.

"I'm sorry, Sue." It wasn't enough, but it was a start.

5. The Camera Club Trophy

Geoff's son-in-law, Neil, poured the champagne he'd ordered for the adults. Geoff filled the children's glasses with sparkling apple juice, which looked exactly the same. He liked the way the cold drinks beaded the glasses with condensation, and he made everyone laugh by insisting on taking a photo. In truth it was his own happiness he was recording. It bubbled and sparkled through him but, as he wasn't transparent, that didn't show, except in his eyes.

"What shall we drink to first, Dad?" Karen asked.

"That's a good question," Neil said. "With so many things to celebrate, perhaps I should have ordered another bottle?"

Geoff glanced at Cynthia's face and knew instantly that the dear, shy lady would rather not be made a fuss of. Just as well perhaps as he couldn't do justice to his emotions through words. "No, no. This is plenty and very generous of you, Neil. And rather than take up the whole evening with toasts and speeches, I think there's one which says it all." He stood and raised his glass. "To photography!"

"To photography," everyone repeated.

"Was that OK?" he said to Cynthia, as he sat down again.

"Perfect."

Geoff Anderson had always enjoyed photography. At first he'd just taken the usual snaps – his family on holidays and his daughter as she grew up, but over the years his interest became a passion. He'd signed up for evening classes and attended workshops which helped him make the most of his equipment and talent.

"Can you take shots for the press release?" he was often asked at work.

"Of course!" And then at home said, "That makes me a semi-professional photographer!"

If anyone got married in the family, although they hired a photographer leaving Geoff free to enjoy the day, they always said they hoped he might take a few pictures. It delighted him that some of his candid shots always made it into the album or were framed and put on the wall.

His interest helped him through Mary's illness. She'd known she didn't have long and it gave her great pleasure to look through his many photos of their family.

"In a way it feels as though I'll still be with you, Geoff my love. I'll live on in memory, on film and in Karen and the grandchildren."

"You will indeed." He said it because it comforted her, but also because it was true. How could she be forgotten when, at any moment, he could open one of his albums and see her infectious smile, or look at his daughter and see the beauty they'd created together.

The Winkleigh Marsh camera club was so important when he was first widowed. He'd moved, with his albums of pictures, to a smaller place near Karen. She'd been wonderful, but had a husband, children and a job so he didn't want to take up too much time. The camera club gave him something to aim for: the Stanley Hammond trophy. It had been presented in 1963 by one of the founder members. Geoff wanted that trophy. Partly as an acknowledgement of his skill and partly because his name would be engraved on it in perpetuity. He'd never minded having a daughter who'd got married and had children who didn't carry his name. They were just as much his family, but it would be nice for the Anderson name to carry on somewhere. Etched into the base of that trophy seemed the perfect place.

Geoff had, coincidentally, joined the camera club on the night the competition entries were handed in. Each entrant was required to submit five prints, all different images of the same subject. He hadn't brought anything suitable with him, so couldn't enter. That didn't matter. What did was that the club provided him with hope – and companionship.

"There are monthly meetings and organised outings," the secretary told him when he'd first enquired.

He'd soon discovered the members often invited each other on days out to take pictures. Geoff, with his comfortable car and willingness to drive, was never short of interesting company and something to do whenever he wanted. Some days Geoff went out with a car full. More often it was just himself and Cynthia, the club's secretary. She lived alone and didn't drive. To be frank she wasn't much of a photographer, but she liked having a go and made rather wonderful picnics.

Geoff entered the trophy competition in his second year as a member of the club. The judge confessed he'd had trouble deciding between Geoff's entry and another. In the end the other, a collection which consisted of baby photos, had won.

"As I was deliberating my son phoned to tell me I was to become a granddad and I'm rather afraid that may have coloured my judgement," the judge admitted.

Geoff couldn't blame the man. He loved his grandchildren and could see how that might sway him. Anyway coming second on his very first attempt was something to be proud of. Truth be told, if he'd won that time it might have seemed a little too easy and not meant so much as it would the following year.

He switched over to a digital camera soon after that. The update was long overdue. Geoff would probably still use blankets instead of a duvet and be without a mobile phone if Mary hadn't convinced him to make the first change and the combined hints and encouragement of Karen and Cynthia persuaded him into the second.

Cynthia used a digital camera and showed him how easy it was to email pictures to friends and family anywhere in the world. Geoff didn't really need to do that thanks to Karen and his grandchildren living so close, but liked the way it pleased Cynthia to help him. He also liked the idea of sending weather pictures into the local television station and showing off his work on the internet – and knew that Cynthia would be a willing teacher.

It took him quite a while to fully get to grips with the new techniques. Because of that, for a time the pictures he produced weren't of his usual high standard. He briefly considered entering a collection of earlier shots into the competition for the Stanley Hammond trophy, but it was an unwritten rule that only current work be submitted and Geoff always played fair.

When a savings scheme he'd almost forgotten about paid out, Geoff asked Karen if there was anything which she or her family needed, or which would make things easier for them.

"There's nothing we need more than seeing you happy, Dad. Why not use it for a special trip to get some great photos?"

His holiday to Sri Lanka was a success in that respect. One day they visited an elephant sanctuary. Geoff asked to stay behind when the rest of the coach party went off to buy souvenirs. That gave him plenty of time to set up his shots exactly how he wanted them and as a bonus the harsh light changed to a rich golden glow as day prepared to slip into night. The light gave his pictures that extra depth, that something magical.

Geoff enjoyed good food, wonderful weather, comfortable accommodation and interesting photographic opportunities. Even so, at times he'd felt something was missing. Or rather someone. Mary? No. Although he often still thought about her, looked at the photos he'd taken of her and remembered with love their time together, he was by then accustomed to the fact she wasn't physically by his side. He missed Karen and her family of course, but when they'd gone away on their own trips he'd not felt this way. Geoff missed his camera club friends too, but the other people on the same itinerary were pleasant and friendly. Two men in particular were only too happy to talk cameras with him. Geoff had been pleased to get home.

A few days before the meeting at which the trophy winner would be announced, the club secretary banged on Geoff's door. When he opened up, she was shaking, unable to speak and looked close to tears.

"Cynthia! Whatever's wrong?" Geoff feared something awful had happened to her and she'd fled to him for shelter. As he gently coaxed the words from her, he discovered the something awful had happened to him.

"Your entry wasn't picked as the winner and I was so sure it should have been I asked the judge why not," she said.

That was such a surprising action for the meek lady that Geoff didn't immediately take in the fact that he'd not won.

"He said he hadn't seen any photos of elephants. I searched my flat and found they'd slipped down the back of a cupboard. I'm so, so sorry."

Geoff couldn't be angry. He was disappointed, no getting away from it, but he saw it was just an accident.

"Don't worry, Cynthia. There's always next year. Come in and I'll put the kettle on."

The winner would be that new lass, Hayley, he was sure. She was studying photography at college, hoping to become professional. Already her work was very promising, sometimes brilliant but not consistently so. That would come if she worked at it and maybe winning the trophy would spur her on.

Geoff was right. Young Hayley did win. When he saw how happy she was it almost wiped away his thought that it should have been him.

By the following year there was only space for one more name to be engraved onto the trophy. It was decided that whoever won it that year should keep it permanently. This was Geoff's last chance. The trophy was to be awarded on his birthday, so it seemed he was almost fated to win. He didn't mention the coincidence of the date though; he didn't want anyone to feel they should bother with cards and all that sort of thing.

"How about we make more of the competition for the final year?" the chairman suggested. "We could all present a larger body of work and vote on who should win the trophy."

"I'm not sure we could ensure entries were anonymous," Cynthia said. "So many of us take pictures together, or know what others are working on."

"True. Maybe we should take the photographer, not just the photography, into account?"

It was agreed. Geoff wasn't sure if that would help his chances or not. He got on with everyone and thought he was fairly well liked in return, but they were a friendly group and the same could be said of most of the others. The idea of an even bigger competition appealed to him regardless of his chances of winning.

"Why don't we hold an exhibition and let others come and see it? We know there will be good work on display," he suggested.

The idea was quickly accepted.

"Perhaps for this, we should select from our very best work whenever it was taken?" Cynthia said.

Geoff was very much in favour of that as it allowed him to enter his elephant photos as well as some more recent efforts. He was very pleased with the selection he put together and proudly hung them in the exhibition before looking at what everyone else had brought.

Everyone's work was of a high standard. Even Cynthia's photography was coming on marvellously under his guidance. It was fascinating to see all the different subjects, and the techniques used to capture them. There were coloured images and arty black and white ones. Photos of entire landscapes and macro close ups of tiny details. There were silhouettes, portraits and action shots. Everyone had reason to be proud of their efforts, but it was obvious some were better than others. Geoff's main rival was Hayley, he felt. Just on the pictures, Geoff thought he might win though he realised it was hard to be objective about his own work – and the pictures weren't the only factor to be considered. Hayley was very pleasant. Her personality wouldn't go against her, and youth was in her favour he thought. Geoff would take more photos and some might be good, but he recognised he'd reached his peak. These days, on club outings, he was less inclined to stand for hours in the freezing cold to get the perfect shot, when he could take a fairly good one then head for the café with Cynthia for a nice hot cup of tea.

Hayley had talent that was increasing day by day. She could become truly great. A lot of club members would vote for her, and Geoff wouldn't blame them. Who would Geoff vote for? Not himself. Maybe no one would know, but they'd agreed not to do that. After all, if they all did then where would they be? He could vote for someone who wasn't a threat to his last chance to get his hands on the trophy or he could do the right thing and vote for Hayley and then most likely have to take a deep breath before congratulating her. As he wrote her name he wondered what she would do and was glad he didn't know.

Hayley won by one vote. His vote he couldn't help thinking, but she was good, there was no shame in coming second to her. Disappointment admittedly, but no shame, and he'd get over it.

When the public were let in to admire the pictures, Geoff's family were first through the doors.

"Yours are best, Granddad," his grandchildren all loyally declared.

"They are, Dad," Karen said. "Though the portrait of you done by the woman who won is wonderful. I'd have voted for her just for that."

"I voted for her despite it," Geoff said with a chuckle. Technically it was excellent, but he was fully aware he wasn't the prettiest of subjects. Still, her shots of the butterflies which had found their way into the flower marquee at the village show made up for that.

The club chairman got everyone's attention by tapping his coffee cup. "Ladies and gentlemen, it's time for the presentations."

Geoff was called forward with Hayley. Of course he was, as he always took the group's pictures to go with any reports Cynthia wrote for local papers. It was a true compliment to be asked by a camera club to take their pictures.

He set up his tripod, then glanced round the room. He was surrounded by friends and family and everyone there had admired and praised his photographs. His name appeared quite often in the paper under a picture and even sometimes on the TV with the weather photos. He didn't need his name on the trophy. He'd have liked it, liked it a lot, but by the time he'd photographed Hayley receiving it and set up the time delay so he could be in the picture of the whole club, his smile was as broad and genuine as that of the winner.

"Just one more presentation to make," the chairman said.

Geoff glanced at the others. No one else was surprised. Was he growing forgetful?

"As the Stanley Hammond trophy has now been presented for the last time, we of course need a new one and I'm delighted to say that one has generously been donated by the friends and family of one of our most popular members."

Geoff tried to keep his face neutral. He definitely hadn't been told about this. He should have been informed. Wasn't he an important member of the club?

"I'd like to ask tonight's winner to present it."

As if that girl hadn't got enough attention already and why was it being presented? No one had won it had they?

"Geoff, set up the timer will you?"

Geoff complied, but he'd rather not have done. Some birthday party this was turning out to be!

The chairman made a speech. "It gives us great pleasure to present this trophy, which in subsequent years will go to the winner of our annual competition. This year though, it seems only right that it grace the home of the person whose name it bears."

Hayley handed the box to Geoff and lifted the lid rather in the manner of a conjurer pulling a rabbit from a hat. The cup was big, plenty of room for winners names to be engraved for decades to come. It was elegantly shaped and highly polished and there, right in the centre were etched the words 'Geoff Anderson Challenge trophy'.

"I don't understand," Geoff said. He looked closer, hoping to make sense of what was happening. Inside the cup were dozens of envelopes bearing his name. Birthday cards, that's what they must be. That was confirmed when everyone sang, 'Happy Birthday' to him.

"You don't let us do much for you," Karen explained, "But we knew you wouldn't mind if we did something for your camera club."

Geoff didn't know what to say, but as he doubted he'd be able to speak without giving way to emotion that was perhaps a blessing.

"Are you taking us out to celebrate, Granddad?" his eldest grandchild asked.

"Yes, of course I am," Geoff said. "I know my birthday is usually a family only event, but would you mind if I asked someone else to join us?" That question was directed at his daughter.

"If it's Cynthia, then we'd be delighted. Actually, don't you think it's about time you made her part of the family?"

Really! Did everyone know everything before he did? He looked over to Cynthia and remembered how lonely he'd felt in Sri Lanka without her by his side to share the view and finally caught up with what should have been obvious to him a long time ago.

"You go on ahead and I'll ask her," Geoff said.

It took him a few moments to make his meaning clear. Perhaps he'd over complicated things by suggesting that she might like her name to become that which was engraved on the new cup. Once Cynthia understood she said, "Of course I'll marry you, Geoff."

As he held Cynthia in his arms he knew he'd remember the moment for a long time, not least because a camera flash alerted him to the fact Hayley had taken their photograph. What a perfect shot that would be – taken by the cup winner and showing the happiness he felt and which was mirrored on Cynthia's face. He'd ask for a copy and give it pride of place in a brand new photo album.

6. Happy Ever After

Mum read loads of books where people got married and lived happy ever after. I wished her life could be like that. She said it couldn't, but I didn't see why.

"We've got a book at school with really weird animals like whales with huge unicorn spikes on their heads that look made up but are called narwals and are real."

"Well, yes."

"And one about a queen who cut off people's heads like Alice in Wonderland and that really happened too."

"True." She was laughing though, like she didn't really believe me.

I fetched the book she'd just read, and pointed out she was just as pretty as the woman on the cover and nowhere near as skinny.

"That's very kind of you, Claudia."

I thought about it for a while. "It's not you that's the problem, is it? It's the men?"

"You're right again. They aren't all like those in books."

I actually thought that was good as they usually didn't look up to much, but I didn't say. "I think it would help if you actually had a boyfriend," I told her.

"Oh you do, do you?"

She did try, I'll give her that, but she didn't have much luck. That's partly my fault. No, not fault exactly. I couldn't help being born and I haven't done anything really mean to them, but her boyfriends often didn't seem keen to have me around and they never passed my tests.

When she hadn't got a boyfriend Mum spent all the time I wasn't at school with me. We did lots of fun things and went to good places but I knew Mum wanted someone to love her like in her books and how Daddy did before he got killed. If it would make Mum happy it was something I wanted too. I understood her boyfriends didn't want to share her. I wasn't especially keen to have anyone taking Mum out places, and away from me, either. I was willing to compromise though, so why weren't the boyfriends?

I wanted a dad to love me too. You can't get a new dad, but Mum could get a new husband. He had to be the right one though.

For a start, he had to be honest, not pretend to like me when really he wanted me to go away. I never pretended to like the men who wanted to be Mum's boyfriend. I tried to like them but, if I didn't, I told the truth.

Some men said, "Here's money for sweets, Claudia," or brought presents or paid for me to go to the pictures. That was OK sometimes but children shouldn't just be bought what they want. I heard Gran tell Mum that. Mum agreed and didn't get me the new trainers I wanted. I tested the boyfriends by pretending to want expensive things. If they just bought them they'd be no good as a stepdad. They should save the money to spend on Mum and tell me it was too expensive, maybe I could have it for my birthday. That's what Mum and Gran did. Then we'd play a game or make cakes or do something that was good but didn't cost lots.

Mum's boyfriend had to be reliable. It was no good promising to do something and then letting us down. If they did, they failed.

Mack didn't look anything like the make believe men in Mum's books. He didn't have such stupid hair. Actually he didn't have any. Nor did he have such big, white teeth that he looked like he'd bite. And he kept his shirt on. All good.

He turned up when he said he would and if he promised to do or fix something, then he did it. He didn't pretend he really wanted me around all the time, then make excuses why I had to stay with Gran. He said straight out that sometimes he'd like to go somewhere just with Mum or he'd like me to stay at Gran's on Saturday, then we could all do something fun on Sunday.

"Is that OK, Claudia?"

I always said it was and I was right. Mum had a good time on her own with Mack and I had fun at Gran's doing stuff like painting Gran's shed to look like a zebra, or helping knit hats for gnomes.

Sometimes Mack gave me pocket money after I'd helped weed the garden, or put away the shopping or washed up. He bought me a Christmas present and sometimes gave me a magazine or bar of chocolate, but not instead of talking to me, or to get rid of me.

Then one day Mack said he needed to talk to me. "I want to marry your mum, Claudia. I think I'd make her a good husband. What do you reckon?"

"Maybe," I said. I thought he would, but couldn't agree. That bit was up to Mum. Mack seemed to expect me to say something else so I asked, "What about me? "

"I can't take the place of your dad. I know you loved him. A stepdad isn't the same, but I think I'd be OK at that."

That seemed OK. I was just going to say so when I remembered I'd never given him a test. I thought I should as this whole getting Mum the right man thing was my idea. I wanted him to pass, so I warned him.

"We can do a test to see if you'd be a good stepdad."

"Umm… OK."

"It's my birthday soon."

He nodded to show he knew.

"You can give me a party. I want it really huge, with hundreds and hundreds of people, music, masses of food, an enormous cake and for it to be toasty warm, really bright and pretty and I want good presents like… diamonds, and for all my friends to be there."

Aware I'd got carried away, I stopped. Obviously I did want a party like that, but it was totally impossible. That was actually the point. He'd have to say no; I was cheating for him. After school it's already dark and it's cold all the time now, so warm and bright was impossible. We've got lights in the house, there wouldn't be room for hundreds of people and all my friends, plus masses of food so it would need to be outside.

I could see him thinking. Come on, hurry up and say you can't do it, then you can ask Mum to marry you and we can all live happy ever after.

"That's your test? I give you a party like that and you let me marry your mum and be your stepdad?"

Noooooo! "Yes."

"OK. Six o'clock on the twelfth of November it is. Be there or be square."

I gave him credit for actually knowing when my birthday was, but that's it. He must have noticed my expression.

"Sorry, that phrase wasn't cool even when I was your age."

I didn't know what to do. My tests had lost Mum boyfriends before. I'm still sure they were no good, but what do I know? I'm only eleven and I can't remember Dad that well. I know what he was like because Mum tells me how lovely he was, but she sounds the same when she talks about Mack.

First I tried to drop hints that he should say no. "Mack doesn't know my school friends, Mum, so he won't be able to invite them."

What she was supposed to do was agree and explain to him he couldn't do it, then he'd tell me and pass the test. Simples.

What she actually said was, "He's thought of that."

He gave me sealed envelopes and told me to write my friends' names on them. I did.

"Please give them out at school and ask them to show their parents but NOT you as it's a surprise party."

I wasn't happy.

My friends all said they could come and thought it would be really good. Even though I begged them to tell me what the invitations said they wouldn't because it was a surprise. My friends are good like that. They would be; I'm a really great judge of character. That's why I knew Mack was good and I shouldn't have given him the test. I felt sick… Yes! That was the answer, I'd say I wasn't well so we had to cancel the party. Then I could tell Mack it wasn't his fault he couldn't do it and he could marry Mum.

I tried, but Mack said that wasn't fair. "We had a deal, Claudia."

Gran drove me to the party. I thought it was a bad sign Mack wasn't there, but good Mum was with him wherever he was. Mum's really clever, perhaps she would think of something.

We met all my friends in the car park. There were loads of other people. Hundreds and hundreds. That was something I'd asked for and so was my friends being there. That was two things. If I added everything up that Mack got right and gave him a point then I could say he had done well enough to pass. People pass tests even if they get some things wrong. I decided if he got twelve points he'd definitely passed the test. That seemed fair as I was twelve that day and the date was the twelfth and with Mum and

Mack and Gran and me and all my friends there were twelve of us.

We walked across a field following the other people. Mum and Mack held up a banner saying "Happy Birthday". Some people going in wished me happy birthday and said how nice to have such an unusual party. I gave Mack a bonus point for that so he was up to three. No four. The people called it a party. It being a party was on the list.

We stood by a big bonfire so it was toasty and warm! Five points. Best of all it was a firework display so it would be bright and pretty. Two more points. Some people walked about with drums and stuff. Guess you could call it music. Eight points.

My friends gave me presents. None were like diamonds, but they were still lovely things; chocolates, hair-slides with tiny goldfish on, a really nice pencil case, a teeny tiny teddy and more chocolates. Nine points. I only said presents, not that Mack needed to buy them.

The fireworks were fab, then we had hot dogs from a stall piled high with masses of bread rolls. Ten points, then eleven when Mack told the hot dog seller I was the birthday girl so he said, "It's safe in the van, mate."

Mack got my birthday cake. He must have asked the man to look after it as it had my name on it and the right number of candles. Come on Mack, just one more point!

Someone asked to see our tickets. He took them and gave us a sparkler each. Sparklers sparkle! Duh, obviously they do that's why they're called sparklers, but diamonds are sparkly and sometimes called sparklers too. This could be the deciding point.

"What a lovely present," I said.

"I don't think they are," one of my friends said. Ex friend at that point, though we've made it up since. "They were included in the ticket."

"Mack gave me my ticket as a present," I snarled.

"Actually this is your birthday present from me," the flipping idiot said. He gave me a voucher saying I could have horse riding lessons. Why couldn't he have just said it was the sparkler? Then he'd have won.

He looked sad. "I know you'd have liked your own pony but I hope this is nearly as good." Aaaargh!!!! Why didn't I make getting me a pony the test? He'd have won easy.

"It's a fab present, thank you." I hugged him and felt like Judas S. Carrot.

"Hey, Claudia what's the matter?"

I was crying. Mum put her arm around me but I pushed her away. I didn't deserve my lovely party and for her to love me when I'd made Mack take a test I knew he'd fail.

"Mack, you've messed everything up," I said, even though it was really my fault. I tried to run away, but he caught me up in like three seconds. I wanted to tell him to forget about the test and that he could marry Mum anyway, but I couldn't. We had a deal.

"Look, Claudia I know I cheated a bit with your party, but we've had fun, haven't we?"

I agreed.

"I know there will be other times I can't do exactly what you want, but I'll always try."

"OK." That seemed reasonable.

"And there might be times I can't do what your mum wants either, but I'll do my best. I love her very much and I am going to ask her to marry me. I'd much prefer to do it with your blessing, but I'm going to do it anyway."

"Thank goodness for that!" He hadn't got all twelve points, but eleven was very close. Eleven days out of twelve being happy ever after would be OK. It would be like a compromise and like real life, not a book. "When were you thinking of asking her?"

"I was going to ask you about that. If you'd agreed today I thought I could ask her straight away, then this would always be a special day for all of us. But it's your birthday, so if you want me to wait until tomorrow I will."

"You should get a ring first, so it better be tomorrow."

"The ring isn't what's worrying me." He showed me a tiny box.

"Can I look."

"Sure."

The ring sparkled in the light from the bonfire.

"Diamonds?"

"Yes. It was your idea. Remember you said you wanted them for your party?"

"Twelve points!" I hugged him.

"What does that mean?" Mum asked. I hadn't even noticed she'd come over. I didn't explain as there was something more important she should listen to, and it was Mack who had to say it. I left them to it and went back to my friends and Gran.

We couldn't hear Mum and Mack because the drumming had started again and we could only see them as silhouettes against the bonfire. Mack sank down on one knee and held out the box. She took it and then it looked like he put the ring on her finger and then they started kissing. Then they did more kissing so I went and stopped them.

"You've got ever after to do that! This is still my birthday and I want you to sing Happy Birthday to me."

They did. We all lived happy ever after.

7. Own Goal

"Aaaargh no!" Jamie kicked his kitbag across the changing room. Just as well he'd not known the decision until after the match or he'd probably have said something to the ref and got a yellow card or worse.

He got that goal but, because it just brushed against an opposing player, he wasn't going to get the credit. It wasn't fair at all. Not to anyone; the other bloke was hardly going to be thrilled he was credited with an own goal and the fans weren't happy either.

None of it was fair. Jamie really struggled to fit football in around the rest of his life. He had to earn a living away from the game so no wonder he wasn't as good as the likes of Cristiano Ronaldo, Lionel Messi and Jamie Vardy who'd had nothing to do but practice since they left school. This Jamie had to work, do the shopping, help around the house. Then his big chance, his little club scraped through the FA cup qualifying rounds and then got drawn against the mighty Arsenal!

The game was televised. Jamie made the starting line up. The ball was passed to him. He took the shot and it went into the back of the net. He scored the equaliser that meant a rematch; the best possible outcome really. They'd get more money, another appearance on TV and it was even possible they'd win. Unlikely, but possible. But still, thanks to Jamie they were still in the competition. This should have been Jamie's chance to get picked by a bigger team, to play professionally. Then glory was snatched from him by that own goal decision.

He'd watched the game afterwards. His wife had recorded it. The commentators were full of praise for his plucky team. The local news coverage was even better. They called his shot on goal 'a brave piece of play'. He could have passed, taken the safe option, but he didn't.

"How many more times are you going to watch that?" Shelley asked.

"You used to be supportive," Jamie whined. She had been too. She went to every game and always said she preferred watching him to any of the professional players. Now she hardly ever came. She said it wasn't a good place for the baby and he knew which of them she'd rather spend time with.

"And you used to be fun to be around. You've got what you said you wanted, so why are you still so miserable?" she asked.

Yeah all right he'd said what he wanted was the chance to play against the big boys and he'd done that. What he'd really wanted though was the chance to play *for* them. Maybe the Arsenal strip was quite literally out of his league, but he reckoned he was good enough for one of the teams nearer the bottom. Hadn't he just proved that?

He wanted to have stories to tell his son. Stories that'd make him proud and he wanted the good wages being a professional footballer could bring. Plastering wasn't a bad job, but he could do better.

"I haven't got what I wanted. I nearly had but it was snatched away from me. Look." He played the footage of his shot again.

When he looked round for her agreement she'd left the room. Clearly she didn't care at all. If he'd got the recognition, and money, he deserved he bet that would have been a different story.

"Jamie," she called, "It's for you."

Oh, she'd gone to answer the phone. Still she was probably glad to get away from the sight of what might have been.

The call was from his team manager.

"Jamie, seems you're a star," the man said.

"Really?" He'd not said anything like that after the match. Rather the opposite actually.

"Yes you're in demand."

Thank goodness! Who wanted him? City? United? He had to ask for the message to be repeated.

"The hospice, Jamie. There's this boy there who used to come to the games when he was stronger. You're his hero and he was thrilled to see you on TV. His parents say it would mean a great deal if you could visit him."

"I don't know." Hospices must be pretty depressing places and making the visit would give him less training time. He had to be at his peak for the replay.

"The request came through the TV company and it'd be good publicity for the team," the manager coaxed.

It might help raise Jamie's profile too. They'd probably show another clip of him in action when they mentioned him and you never knew who could be watching.

"OK, I'll do it."

Shelley was far more enthusiastic than he was.

"What a lovely thing to do. That poor boy will be thrilled to meet a real life football star I'm sure."

So now she decided to treat him like a hero! Well it seemed he was to someone, even if it wasn't one of the people who mattered, those who could do him some good.

The phone rang again. This time the call was from his young teammate, Terry.

Jamie had to listen to his excited burbling for quite a while before he understood Terry had been offered a contract with a bigger club and, as long as his medical checks were OK, would become a professional footballer.

"I can't tell you how thrilled I am," he gasped.

He didn't need to, Jamie could guess exactly how happy he was. He tried to be happy for his friend. Tried without much success

Terry said, "This is my dream come true."

It had been Jamie's dream too, but it wouldn't come true for him. Terry would likely be unbearable now, thinking he was better than the rest of them.

Jamie studied his goal yet again. The sick kid would be bound to want him to talk it through. He watched as the ball came to him. He hadn't really had a clear shot. Terry had. Terry had been looking for the pass. It would have been easy for Jamie to flick him the ball and Terry would have scored. Could hardly have missed from there. Some might say that's what he should have done. Their manager had.

Jamie scored though, didn't he? The result was the same for the team he argued with himself. It was, but only because it deflected off the other player. It really had been an own goal. Jamie hadn't been robbed, but he'd robbed Terry of his chance to score and almost robbed his team of a chance at a rematch. He was no hero.

He cringed as he watched his goal celebration and remembered how he'd talked to the others as though he'd been the only one playing and they all owed him. He'd forgotten football was a team game.

Marriage was a team game too and he'd not played fair with Shelley lately either. His wife had always supported him and still did. She looked after the boy and house while he practised, and always had his dinner waiting when he came home muddy and too tired to be good company. She'd made sacrifices for him by giving up her career to have his baby, he saw that now. She'd even agreed to his choice of name for their little one, despite wanting to call him after her father. He saw she wouldn't want to move away, to be in the spotlight like the 'WAGS' who were often seen on TV. Not that Jamie ever really had the kind of talent which would make that happen. If he had, he'd have been selected as a teenager just like young Terry.

Jamie was no hero and didn't deserve to be thought of as one. There were others who did, some of whom he owed an apology. Shelley for a start.

She forgave him the minute he mumbled, "Sorry I've been moody."

"I expect you're tired, what with working and practising."

"I expect you are too what with looking after little Yaya with no help from me."

"Well..."

"I'll take him out for a few hours tomorrow, give you a break."

Ensuring Shelley had some time to herself really was his main motive, but there were other advantages to taking the baby with him. Firstly it ensured his manager didn't yell at him for his selfish play, when Jamie called round to see him.

"I was wrong," Jamie said. "It won't happen again."

"It better not. Doubt we'd get away with such stupidity again."

Yaya made a strange gurgling sound just then which made them both laugh. When Jamie left half an hour later the two men were once again on good terms.

Next Jamie called in on Terry to congratulate him properly. "You deserve it lad. Still I reckon you owe me?"

"I do, yeah. You've helped me and I'm grateful," Terry said.

"That's not what I meant. More that playing alongside an obvious amateur like me was bound to make you look good."

Terry's mum came into the room then, wanting to fuss over Yaya. She offered tea and home made cake in exchange for a cuddle.

"You'll miss her cooking when you join your club," Jamie pointed out.

"I'll miss a lot of things. But…"

"Oh you're doing the right thing lad, don't worry. Just wish there could be two of us doing that."

After he'd eaten two slices of Terry's mum's legendary lemon drizzle cake, Jamie went home and started calling other players. It took him a few days to get round everyone, but he felt a lot better when he had. Finally he rang the lady at the hospice.

"It's about my visit to see little Peter. There's been a change of plan."

"Please don't let him down, we can reschedule if the date is difficult. He's been so looking forward to it. We all have."

"Oh I'm coming, just not on my own. I'll be bringing my team mate, Terry too. You may have seen on the news that he's been asked to train for one of the big clubs?"

"Yes. Oh that's wonderful!" She almost shrieked with enthusiasm.

"And a few of my other team mates would like to come."

"Great. The more the merrier. Quite a few of our residents are football fans."

"Good, because I've asked the opposition team if any of them can make it and some said yes."

"Opposition? You don't mean…?"

"Yes, Arsenal."

"But they're in the premiership and…"

Dave wasn't sure if she'd stopped talking or if excitement had made her voice so high he could no longer hear it. "My manager will call to make the final arrangements."

The visit, Jamie learned, would be televised. It was originally going to be all about him, but with the other, far more high profile, players in attendance thanks to him, he'd probably not even get a mention.

In a way that might be seen as a different type of own goal. Jamie knew it wasn't, that this time he was doing the right thing. A sick child and some of his friends would be happy and he'd be proud to be part of the team making that happen.

8. The Right Position

As Elizabeth reached Ulrika's domestic service agency another young woman raced out.

"What's up with her?" Elizabeth asked Ulrika.

"The usual – Mr Jouy. She won't be coming back."

The agency's meanest client had claimed another victim. It wasn't just the girl who'd quit who was upset. Ulrika herself looked close to tears. Elizabeth made her a cup of tea.

"You're a good girl, Elizabeth."

Elizabeth was fed up with being good. Because she was so easy going and never complained Ulrika relied on her as a temp and didn't offer the permanent position Elizabeth wanted. Ulrika was far too busy and sometimes bookings got overlooked. Elizabeth was often called, when she was expecting the day off or even to go on holiday, and persuaded to come in. Elizabeth never said no to anybody who asked for help.

Yesterday for example her sister, Valerie, begged Elizabeth to look after baby Harry. "My baby sitter has let me down at the last minute."

"I've got a really early start tomorrow…"

"I could bring the baby round to you and collect him really early in the morning, whatever time you like. Please, Sis. I hardly ever get an evening out."

That was true. "OK."

Valerie did pick up her son at the time agreed and gave Elizabeth a lift to near her latest job.

"Is here OK?"

"It's fine. You'll get caught up in the one-way system if you go any closer."

51

It would have been fine if little Harry hadn't thrown up on her as she bent to kiss him good-bye.

Elizabeth ran down the street to her appointment and collided with a man, transferring baby puke from her sweater onto his smart jacket. He seemed quite nice from what she could tell as she hastily dabbed at the baby sick on his lapel.

"So sorry," she muttered before rushing off to her appointment.

"Good of you to agree to the early start," her client, a harassed mother of triplets, said when Elizabeth arrived.

By the time she'd cleaned, dressed and fed the toddlers, Harry's vomit didn't show at all. Helping her sister hadn't done Elizabeth any harm. In an optimistic frame of mind she called in to see Ulrika.

"It's a shame I couldn't contact you earlier, a permanent position came up but I've filled it already."

Great! The only reason Ulrika couldn't contact her was because she'd taken the demanding job with the triplets as a favour.

She didn't learn her lesson though. On her way home she stopped to help a woman whose shopping bag split. As a result, Elizabeth was drenched by a car splashing at speed through a puddle. The woman shopper was very apologetic and asked Elizabeth to come into her house which was nearby and dry off.

"I'll be fine thanks, anyway I have a bus to catch."

She arrived at the stop just as the bus left, meaning she had almost an hour wait for the next one. She started shivering almost immediately. After a few minutes a car pulled up and baby sick man from that morning offered her a lift. He still seemed nice, but she sensibly and politely said, "No thanks, the bus will be here soon."

Soon she wished she'd taken a chance on him being an axe murderer. At least she'd have had a warm death.

She'd only just got in and changed when her elderly neighbour called round.

"Please come and help. Tiddles is stuck in the tree again."

Elizabeth would rather have left the spiteful thing up there, it would come down of its own accord when it got hungry. She couldn't; her neighbour was convinced Tiddles was frightened and became distressed herself. Elizabeth climbed up for her sake. Her reward was vicious scratches and a message to say she had a job interview on Monday.

She hoped that when she got there the mother would be the woman she'd helped with the shopping bags or Tiddles' owner would turn out to be the children's grandmother and they'd be delighted to employ her. As long as the dad wasn't baby sick man, who she'd treated like a potential kidnapper, she had a chance.

He wasn't. She hadn't met anyone in the house before. The interview seemed to go well until she stretched out her arm to accept a cup of tea. Even then if she'd simply explained the cat scratches instead of blushing, stuttering and pulling down the thick cardigan she was wearing on a sunny day, it wouldn't have looked so bad.

Oh well, it had only been a temporary position anyway.

Elizabeth returned to the agency.

"Sorry, dear, " Ulrika said. "I don't have anything else suitable at the moment."

"I'll do anything."

"Well… A gentleman has asked us to find him a permanent nanny."

"Why didn't you say so?"

"It's Mr Jouy."

"No, not him!"

"His wife has left him apparently. I think she was partly the cause of the trouble, maybe things will be better now?"

"I don't know."

"He says he'll keep the nanny he gets, he doesn't want the children upset anymore."

That sounded hopeful. From what she'd heard, the needs of his children were very low down on his priorities. Maybe she'd been wrong to believe the gossip – and this was an offer of a permanent position.

"Say you'll go to the interview at least," Ulrika pleaded.

Elizabeth gave in. By the time she arrived at the huge house with its impressive gardens she'd decided she wanted the job. As she was early, the housekeeper first showed Elizabeth the spacious rooms she'd be given.

"You get use of the car too, whenever you like."

Elizabeth was shown into the library to meet her prospective employer. It was baby sick man. No way would he give her a job. At least that meant she was no longer nervous. She just wanted to get through the interview and leave as soon as possible.

He shook her hand. Instead of releasing it, he twisted her arm to look at the scratches. Elizabeth explained about Tiddles.

He gestured for her to take a seat. Her chair was low and hard. His was higher and looked comfortable. On the table by his side was a single cup of coffee and plate of biscuits.

"Good with animals are you?" He didn't wait for her reply. "That's excellent. We have three dogs and they need a lot of exercise."

Why was he telling her? She was applying to be a nanny not a kennel maid. Still, she did like animals and found herself saying she'd help out as needed. True, she'd promised herself to stop letting people walk all over her, but it was hard to break old habits and anyway, there was no harm in being agreeable as there was no chance she'd get the job.

"I'm glad you didn't get in my car when I offered you a lift."

No hope he hadn't recognised her then. She waited as he dunked a biscuit and ate it.

"Some people are far too trusting. I've got a lot of valuable antiques here, wouldn't want any gullible staff letting crooks into the house to steal them."

Was she to be security officer as well as kennel maid then? She noticed his concern wasn't that she or the children might come to harm.

He explained what was to be expected of her in terms of timekeeping, not disturbing him and keeping receipts for anything she bought. There was no mention of how she was to care for the children, anything about their specific needs or suggestion that she should meet them before he made a decision.

"And you'll get one weekend off in three."

That wasn't right. Ulrika had forwarded his email and it clearly said she was to work one weekend in three. Again she didn't get to reply because he went on to say what her salary would be. The amount named was several thousand less than he'd originally offered.

She had to interrupt him telling her that she'd have to provide her licence before she could take the car, to question him about the pay.

"I said up to that amount."

"Yes, but I have every qualification you asked for and more besides. I have excellent references and have shown that I'm willing to be flexible and carry out extra duties as required."

Maybe she'd been too eager to please? Too flexible and he'd seen, and treated, her as a doormat? Well she wasn't having it. She very politely said she'd think about it and let him know.

"No good, I need an answer now." It wasn't just his tone which was bullying, he'd stood up and towered over her.

"Then it's a no."

She rushed back to agency to explain to Ulrika. Too late of course, because he'd already phoned to complain about her.

"Said you were late, looked like you'd been in a fight, had been awkward and were rude."

"It's not true, Ulrika – honestly."

"I know, love and I told him so. He's withdrawn his custom."

"I'm so sorry."

"I'm not. We're well shot of him. He's lost me some of my best girls. Not you though, I hope?"

"No! I want to stay if you've got a job for me?"

"I have, now that I've seen you can stand up for yourself when you have to. This job needs someone as willing and flexible as you, but they can't be a complete pushover."

"I'm not. Not any more. What's the job?"

"My assistant. How do you feel about that? A full time position, mostly based here, but you would have to do a few temporary jobs for our best clients if we couldn't get anyone else, so we didn't have to let them down."

"And my salary? I'd want as much as Mr Jouy was offering."

"You'll get it and a small amount of commission."

"Great. I'll start now shall I? I want to be the one who deletes that man's name from your, rather our, records."

9. Fixed Up

"That's Mike over there," Dorinda said. "What do you think?"

Looking in the direction her friend was pointing, Cassie spotted a pleasant looking man with freckles and sandy hair, who barely matched her own five foot five inches.

"Um, he's, umm…" Her hesitation wasn't so much to do with Mike's rather ordinary appearance as the fact she recognised him. Hard not to when he'd been at every party or social event Cassie had attended in recent weeks. Whenever she'd caught sight of him he'd been surrounded by a group of laughing friends.

Mike being sociable and popular wasn't a problem exactly. Not unless Cassie's suspicions were correct and Dorinda was trying to get the two of them together. Ever since Dorinda had moved in with Bill, she'd been dropping hints along that line.

"I want you to be as happy as me, Cass," she'd said. "To have someone who makes me feel the way I do with Bill."

That was fine in theory. Bill was outgoing, entertaining and generous. He was spontaneous, lively, fun. Absolutely perfect for Dorinda.

Trouble was Dorinda didn't seem to realise the kind of man who made her pulse race with excitement would have Cassie's pounding in nervous alarm. Mike was Bill's brother and Dorinda had assured her that although he lacked a few of his brother's inches, his personality didn't come up short. It was the combination of these good points and the way Dorinda mentioned them so frequently, along with the fact that Mike was inexplicably single, which had Cassie worried. That and Dorinda being practically impossible to say no to.

They'd met at junior school. Dorinda had raced out onto the playground yelling, "Come and play everyone!"

Cassie, following after her, had picked up Dorinda's dropped hair ribbon and returned it.

"Thanks. We're best friends now." She'd immediately begun to swing her skipping rope around the two of them and they'd jumped in unison.

It had been like that ever since. Dorinda was the one who had ideas, started things, took centre stage. Cassie formed the supporting cast. She'd been happy joining in childhood games and perfectly content to tag along to pubs, clubs and parties, as they grew up. Cassie enjoyed listening to the chatter and music, but couldn't start a conversation herself or get up and dance until there were so many others on the floor that she felt more conspicuous sitting down.

Since their teens, Dorinda always had a boyfriend, but she still made time for Cassie. They even double dated a few times. The boys Dorinda attracted were very like her and as a result no one noticed that Cassie barely said a word.

Even when Dorinda's relationship with Bill became serious, it didn't alter the friendship between the girls. They went out together, or stayed in chatting or watching a film, when Bill was at rugby practice or drinking with his team mates. Cassie joined her friend in cheering him on at matches and occasionally the three of them shared a meal.

Of course Dorinda and Bill spent a lot of time on their own and that was fine. Much as Cassie enjoyed being with Dorinda, she liked time away from her too. A chance to sit still and be quiet. To shut out reality and lose herself in a book. The same would be true of a man like Mike; she'd need more time away from him than was compatible with a long term relationship. Why put herself through all the pressure and angst if there was no chance of a happy ever after? Plus, as he was Bill's brother, it would be hard to avoid him after it all went wrong. That would be horribly awkward.

None of this seemed to have occurred to Dorinda and she jumped and waved until Mike detached himself from his friends and came over to be introduced.

He gave Cassie a lovely smile. "Nice to finally meet, after hearing so many good things about you," he said.

So, it wasn't just her who'd been on the receiving end of either Dorinda or Bill's hints that they should get together. Luckily Mike seemed no more convinced than she was that they were perfectly suited and, after a few words of polite conversation, he slipped away.

That didn't deter the matchmakers. Over the next few weeks, Cassie often encountered Mike at her friend's home, or places they went together. He was always pleasant to her, but generally kept a good distance between them and always switched the conversation if either Dorinda or his brother seemed to be leading it into awkward territory.

Those meetings weren't too difficult. She found that Mike's remarks often provoked a burst of conversation from anyone else present and all she had to do was smile, nod and occasionally add a word of agreement to seem to be taking part.

That didn't help when she bumped into Mike in the bookshop. She'd come to like him and naturally didn't wish to appear rude, so gathering her courage she approached and asked how he was.

"Fine. You too, I hope?"

"Yes."

"Good."

At that point the assistant finished serving another customer. "Hi, Cassie. I've put by a couple of books I think you might be interested in." She gestured to a shelf behind the counter.

"No need to ask if you come here often then," Mike said.

"No. I mean yes, I do."

"More of a Kindle man myself, but I wanted to get something for Mum's birthday. Haven't got a clue though."

"You could give her a book token?"

"They still make those?"

Cassie nodded.

"I will then. Good idea. Thanks."

He'd bought his tokens and a card before Cassie finished looking through the books which had been set aside for her consideration. Even so, he hadn't left the shop by the time she'd paid for the three she wanted.

"Do you have time for a coffee?" Mike asked.

"Well, I…"

"Please."

Again Cassie nodded. And again when the lad in the coffee shop said, "your usual?" as they reached the counter.

She even managed to smile at Mike and say, "I come here quite often, too." She accepted Mike's offer of cake; it would give her something to hide behind and an excuse not to say much.

They smiled at each other, sipped their drinks and nibbled their cakes for a few minutes.

A couple of times she thought he was about to speak. At last he blushed and said, "Cassie, this is a bit awkward, but… well, I think Bill and Dorinda are trying to fix us up."

"I think so too."

"You seem nice, but I can see we're very different and it wouldn't work out."

"That's what I thought," she mumbled into her cherry sponge.

When she glanced up, he looked so relieved. "So, we're allies?"

Cassie nodded yet again and as he offered his hand, she shook it.

"We should tell them, I suppose," he said.

"I have tried, but it's hard to dissuade Dorinda once she gets an idea into her head."

"Bill's as bad."

"I think they only talk each other out of things by coming up with an even wackier scheme. Maybe that's what we need?" Cassie suggested. With the pressure off, and a common purpose, talking to Mike wasn't really so difficult.

"OK. So, how about… Next time they try, we pretend to go along with it and fall for each other. We'd have to go out a few times to make it look convincing, but maybe's there's a film or something we'd both like to see so it's not too dreadful. Then we break up in some spectacular fashion and are so broken hearted they never try again?"

"I wouldn't want to make them feel bad." Neither could she imagine herself doing anything in a spectacular fashion.

"No, of course not. So, not broken hearted, we'll just let them see that we're not really suited?"

"OK. Yes." And hopefully Dorinda would also realise that her and Bill's other friends were equally unsuitable as boyfriends for Cassie and this situation wouldn't arise again.

The first part of their plan went extremely well and was actually rather fun. She and Mike, when they were next pushed together, found a quiet corner and gazed into each other's eyes. They grinned conspiratorially, checked for when they were being watched and put on a bit of a performance. Even to her it seemed almost real. Except Cassie wouldn't have been able to think of anything much to say, nor been brave enough to occasionally touch his arm in a flirtatious manner if he'd really been chatting her up.

As Mike suggested, they saw a film together. Neither said much as they watched, as both had read the book and were eager to see how it matched up.

"I recognised the character names, but that was about it!" Mike said afterwards.

"Be fair, they only changed three parts of the story," Cassie replied.

"You think?"

"Yep. Beginning, middle and end!"

His snort of laughter was very unlike his usual controlled chuckles. "OK, you got me there."

"Why don't people just write new stories, if they don't like the originals?" Cassie asked.

"Beats me. Mind you, it's even worse when they change history or the characters of real people."

"That makes me so mad!"

They'd walked to the pub, had three drinks each, two rounds of sandwiches and shared the last slice of Black Forest Gateau, before they'd named all the most terrible examples they could think of and devised suitable punishments for the scriptwriters responsible.

When Mike walked her home he said, "How about we go for a proper meal on Saturday, instead of risking whatever the Red Lion has left?"

She temporarily forgot why he was asking and was delighted he wanted to see her again. "I'd like that, but I promised Dorinda I'd go to the rugby club with her and

Bill." Saying their names reminded her this date had just been for their benefit.

"Oh, yes. The reception their sponsors have organised. I'd forgotten about that. See you there then."

"OK. Bye then." She rushed in before her disappointment became obvious and embarrassed them both.

She felt better the following day when Mike sent a text thanking her for her company and suggesting he pick her up on Saturday. OK, she realised why, but it would still be nice to chat to him on the drive there and home again.

She texted back, *'Good idea. That will help convince D & B we're together.'*

Mike made sure to monopolise Cassie's attention during the rugby club event. It wasn't difficult for her to play her part; Mike was fun. During the dull speeches he entertained her with daft jokes, generally at his own expense and all whispered in her ear. Even better, on the way home he suggested an alternative date for them to go out for dinner.

Cassie took care not to make him feel uncomfortable by seeming too eager. "Actually I'm supposed to be seeing Dorinda then too, but yes, let's go out then. Standing her up can be part of the payback for fixing me up with you."

"Right. Yes, teach her a lesson." He sounded hurt.

Oh dear. In trying to hide how keen she was to see him again, she'd made it seem as though she'd really rather not. "I'm sorry... I didn't... I…"

"Cassie, it's OK." He reached over and squeezed her hand. "I understand."

Neither of them had been to the Greek restaurant before, nor knew much about it, but they couldn't have chosen anywhere better to avoid the evening becoming awkward. Alexandros' Taverna had that night been open for exactly a year and the manager was marking the anniversary. The place was packed and the atmosphere celebratory. The food was served in lots of tiny courses, very tasty and beautifully presented. That gave them a safe topic of conversation, though it was hardly needed. Throughout the meal there was a great deal of bouzouki playing, folk singing and dancing, even some plate smashing. Although that last one seemed to have been an accident on the part of a rushing waiter, it was enthusiastically applauded.

On the way home, Mike said, "I've heard that plate smashing used to be traditional at Greek dinners, but didn't think I'd ever see it happen."

"Me neither. Everyone seemed to enjoy it didn't they? I hope that means the waiter won't get into trouble."

"I shouldn't think he will. Cassie, talking of breaking things…"

Oh no! She knew they'd be staging a break up soon, but was hoping they'd go out at least once more first.

"Do you know why Bill and Dorinda were so keen to persuade you to go out with me?" Mike asked.

"They just wanted us to be as happy as them and couldn't see we're too different for that to work."

"Yeah… That's what I thought."

Why prolong the agony by going over it again? "So, how do we show them they were wrong?"

"We don't. I've already told them," Mike said.

"Oh." It was for the best she supposed. Cassie was too shy and quiet for someone like Mike, except that she wasn't so much when she was with him. And was he quite so outgoing as he seemed or did he, like her, smile and nod on the edges of a group? She'd heard him start off conversations, by soliciting opinions, but she couldn't recall him taking part in the resulting debates other than when he'd been talking to her alone.

It was Cassie who'd approached him in the bookshop. At all those clubs and parties where she'd seen him laughing with friends, she'd been doing the same, hadn't she?

"What did they say?" Cassie asked.

"That I was talking rubbish. That they'd known us a very long time and know what we're really like. They have a point, don't they?" Mike took her hand and continued, "I mean, you prefer paperbacks and I love my Kindle, but we both read the same books."

"And you favour green and I go for black, but we both have a thing for olives."

"Exactly."

"But… you… I thought… What did you mean when you said 'talking about breaking things'?"

"I was trying to confess that this conversation took place before our first date and… I was in on the fixing up."

"Oh!"

"So I can't very well tell them it was a bad idea, can I? Not even if I wanted to."

"I suppose not. Guess we'll have to stay together forever?" Cassie asked.

"Forced into it, I reckon," Mike said.

"Only in the film version."

"Ah, the book might end differently?" Mike asked. "True. 'They all lived happily ever after' is traditional."

"I do like a bit of tradition."

"Me too," Mike said.

"Um, I believe kissing is also traditional at this point."

"I thought you were supposed to be the shy one?" Mike said, but not for quite some time.

---

10. Jack And Jill

Jill strode down the corridor, tapped on the door marked 'Jack Frost', waited for his reply and stepped into her boss's office.

"Ah, Miss Chill, prompt as ever. Do take a seat."

"What's this all about, sir? You sounded quite upset on the intercom."

"I have bad news for everyone. As my deputy I thought you should be the first to know."

"Yes, sir." Jill tried to keep her voice icy calm but inside she was shivering. She loved her job and was very fond of her boss. She didn't want there to be a problem with either.

"Please call everyone for a meeting at midday, then come back and I'll brief you personally."

"Everyone, sir? Even the Imps and Fairies?"

"Yes, Miss Chill, even the Icicle Making and Positioning Section and Frost And Icy Rain Engineering Services."

That's when Jill realised things were serious. Usually the use of departmental nicknames made Mr Frost smile, though he sometimes reprimanded her for the informality. Today he hadn't even noticed, besides everyone knew that whenever the Imps were involved there was trouble. She rushed away to set up the meeting. The sooner she did that the sooner she would receive her briefing and could try to sort out what was wrong.

First she visited the offices of the Eleven Snow Sprinklers. Originally there were twelve Elves, but the department downsized a few years ago. Next she stopped by the department for Triangulation of Lightning. Once there had been eight Trolls, now there were just two. The company had changed a lot since she'd started working there. Some departments had shut down. Once humans invented air travel and could experience any weather any time of year the Sylphs and Angels were no longer required. Fortunately the business of weather forecasting had become more important and most of the staff had received training about pixels, isobars and electronic systems and formed a new department; Pixies. As glaciers melted the Giants had merged with the Dwarves, although luckily most of the job losses there were from voluntary early retirement. Even so, Jill realised Winter Weather plc was a smaller company than it had once been.

Jill was so lost in thought she bumped into the head of the Sparkly Pattern Rapid Implementation Team who was rushing down the narrow passageway.

"What's up with you, Jill?" he asked. "Your face is nearly as long as Gerald's."

Jill tried to pull herself together. If she walked around looking like the man in charge of the Gloomy Nights and Overcast Mornings Environmental Section she'd get everyone really worried.

"Oh, just thinking about something. Glad to see you though, you're a hard man to catch up with."

"What can I do for you?"

"The boss has called a meeting for all staff at midday in the wind tunnel. Can you and the Sprites please attend?"

"No problem. I'm actually just on my way to see Gerald, so I'll let him and the other Gnomes know."

Jill raced, on shaky legs, back to Jack Frost's office. Outside she took a few deep breaths and smoothed her hair. Mr Frost insisted his staff looked calm at all times. Jill tapped on the door and waited. There was no reply, so she tapped again. Still no reply so she opened the door a fraction and glanced in.

Mr Frost was slumped over his desk, quietly moaning.

She ran to him. Jill hardly hesitated before she put her arm around his shoulders. "What's wrong, Mr Frost?"

"Oh, Miss Chill, everything is wrong." He burst into tears, almost as though the warmth of Jill's kindness had melted him.

She hugged him until he regained control, then fetched water from the fridge and coaxed him to drink a little.

"I'm sorry about that," he mumbled then blew his nose and pulled himself together. "Miss Chill, with deep regret I must inform you that our company is being closed down."

"No!"

"I'm sorry. I've done everything I can to keep us going, but there's nothing more I can do. Global warming, increased expectations of humans and Charles Dickens have done for us."

"Global warming I can understand, but not the other two. Don't humans want us now?"

"Some still appreciate the changing seasons, admire the beauty of frost and snow and enjoy snuggling up together on cold dark nights, but many more do not. They want to eat strawberries all year round, take holidays with guaranteed sunshine and automatically switch on the central heating as soon as the nights start to draw in."

"I suppose… But Charles Dickens, how can you blame him? He was the making of us."

"For a time his stories of morals and white Christmases did make us popular. The company expanded dramatically when we won the contract for Christmas sparkle but things have changed now. Many people no longer enjoy snow, claiming it stops all travel and businesses so we've cut right back on that. They aren't so bothered about the inconvenience of frost now they have thermal clothing, cars with heating and hot food in minutes but neither do they care for its beauty."

"So what can we do?"

"Nothing."

"Oh yes we can! We'll still have winter weather, but instead of having it at the traditional time in a short sharp rush, we'll spread it out a bit. The first frost and snow can come later, we'll carry on icy spells well past Easter and throw in plenty of grey days, hailstones and heavy showers throughout the summer."

"We could I suppose. Spreading the winter weather out would make things easier, but it won't solve the Christmas issue."

Jill almost danced on the spot with excitement as she formed her plans and tried to communicate them to Mr Frost. "It will, or at least it could. We could leave Autumn alone and then we'd still have months to put the sparkle back into Christmas."

"Nice try, but people want electronic games not snowball fights. They want tinsel and lights, not frost patterns. They want diamonds in place of icicles, gifts sprinkled with glitter rather than made with love…"

"I know they do," Jill interrupted. "At least some of them do. We'll diversify and educate."

"Diversify into what? Educate who?"

"We'll diversify into creating a recession instead of cold winters. We'll teach humans to appreciate what they have. It'll be hard work for us and a hard lesson for them, but I think it'll work."

"We've got nothing to lose," Mr Frost admitted. When he addressed the staff meeting, instead of saying Winter Weather plc was to close down, he told the Elves, Trolls and Imps, Gnomes, Sprites and Fairies that there were to be major changes and handed over to Jill.

Miss Chill took a deep breath, stood tall and explained her plans for the redistribution of winter weather resources and salvation of Christmas. As they listened and understood the seriousness of the situation, you could have heard a snowflake fall in the conference room.

On Christmas morning, Jill strode down the corridor, tapped on the door marked 'Jack Frost' and entered her boss's office.

"Ah, Miss Chill, prompt as ever. Do take a seat."

"What's this all about, sir? You sounded quite excited on the intercom."

"Look." He pointed to the bank of monitors on the wall. "Your plan has worked, Jill."

Jack Frost and Jill Chill gazed through ice covered windows of human homes. They saw handmade cards strung across walls and inexpensive, but lovingly chosen, gifts heaped on the floor. Even the homes of the frail or frantically busy gleamed where friends, family and neighbours had helped prepare them for the festive season. The eyes of those who were usually lonely sparkled with joy as they made the most of unexpected invitations for a drink or a meal. Tears glistened on the cheeks of people laughing over shared jokes. Everything sparkled.

"Well done, Jill. You've saved Christmas. Now take some time off to enjoy it."

"Thank you, sir, but I'll stay if you don't mind. I have work to do." She'd just remembered there was a leap year coming up and she had plans to ensure the last day of February was the coldest on record. That, she was sure, was the best way to warm the heart of Jack Frost. Out she walked with a spring in her step.

11. Meeting Angel

"I like you a lot… but …"

George scrambled to his feet, slipping the ring into his pocket. "Right, well let's go…" He stopped; guessing she wouldn't want to eat with him now. "Three Crowns?"

Janie gave a small nod.

It wasn't too late to cancel the table he'd booked. He'd left time to cross the park and tell Janie's parents they were engaged and perhaps meet little Angel. George stifled a sigh which was halfway to becoming a sob.

He bought Janie a glass of wine, and an orange juice for himself.

"I'll be back in a minute." He'd cancel the restaurant booking and take a few moments to pull himself together. He kissed her cheek.

"George, I'm so sorry …"

"It's OK," he said.

It wasn't. Nobody wants a 'but' in reply to their proposal. George was even less keen to hear what might have come after it.

It might be how he looked; six foot six, broad and dark. That seemed to make him a good short term boyfriend, excellent pub bouncer and an ideal builder's mate. It apparently made him unsuitable meet the parents, or work in many of the places he'd applied to. He wasn't told that, but saw it in the interviewer's eyes. Feeling it was a lost cause before he'd begun hadn't improved his performance.

Had he done the same thing with Janie? No, not at first. He remembered her from school. She was even prettier six years later. When he'd approached, offering to buy her a drink, he saw she recognised him. She'd accepted the drink and said 'yes' when he asked to see her again.

Things had gone well, until he suggested meeting each other's family. She'd come to lunch with his parents several times and they'd got on. When it came to him meeting her family, there was always an excuse. He'd eventually met her parents, briefly. He'd liked them. They'd either thought he was OK, or were too polite to show their dismay. Janie hadn't introduced him to her daughter. Didn't talk about her, as though she couldn't even have them together in her mind.

George tried to show he was good with children, by telling her about days out with his nephews. That had made her uncomfortable. Why?

George had seen Angel. She was the sweetest kid, with long blonde hair and delicate features worthy of her name. It had been accidental. He'd decided to surprise Janie with a bunch of flowers and seen her pushing her chair up the path. By the time he reached the door himself, there was no sign of the child and Janie never mentioned her. George wouldn't have known the child existed if an old school friend hadn't told him.

Inside the pub, Janie rang her mum. "George just proposed."

"That's wonderful, love! Can we all come and celebrate?"

"There's no celebration. I said no."

"You love him, don't you?"

"Yes."

"And he's a good man, would make a good husband and father."

"In the right circumstances. Why would he want a wife who'd kept a huge part of her life a secret, or to raise a child who's own father couldn't care less?"

"Because she's yours and because he's a good man. Wait… He still doesn't know about Angel?"

"Not even that she exists. I've probably lost him because I didn't tell the truth."

"Where are you?"

"Three Crowns."

"Stay there, OK?"

What an idiot she'd been. If only she'd told George about Angel earlier on, he might have come round to the idea. No way could she have accepted his proposal and then sprung it on him.

She took a small sip of her wine and then a big, deep breath. She'd go and tell him the truth. If he loved her as much as she loved him, then maybe he'd give her a second chance.

Angel was really excited to be going out so late. And to a pub! She'd never been in one before. Even better she was going to meet Mummy's boyfriend George. Mummy said he was really nice and kind and funny. She really, really wanted to meet him.

Granny hadn't meant that about banging some sense into Mummy's head had she? No she can't have, because that would hurt and Granny didn't do hurting people. So that might mean she didn't mean the bit about George being her daddy afterwards either. Shame as she'd like a daddy. She still wanted to meet George though. Maybe he'd like her and want to be her daddy anyway? It was worth a try, wasn't it?

"Hold on a minute," Granny said. She left Angel with Grandad and went to talk to a man in a car.

The man got out. Gosh he was 'normous!

"Angel darling, this is George."

He knelt down in front of her. "Hello, Angel."
"Hello. You're Mummy's boyfriend, aren't you?"
"Yes, I am."
"Do you love her lots and lots?"
"Yes, I do."
"I'm nice too."
"I'm sure you are."
Hooray her plan was working already! She'd sing him a song, everyone liked singing.

Janie left the pub to find George on his knees in front of Angel's wheelchair, being enthusiastically serenaded. As her daughter belted out the words to 'Let it Go' she saw both that she never wanted to let go of her relationship with George and that perhaps she might not have to. Her parents were there and had no doubt introduced Angel and George and would have explained who she was.

George saw her and his expression wasn't one of accusation or reproach but, unless it was wishful thinking on her part, of love and hope.

Janie placed a hand on his shoulder. "Don't get up." As Angel continued to sing, Janie knelt beside him and whispered, "That ring… Maybe I could try it on for size?"

Perhaps it wouldn't fit straight away. Maybe it would need a bit of adjustment, some getting used to, but she'd find a way to make it right.

12. Bags

Christmas is all about bags. There's bags of presents and food to buy. Bags of washing my student kids bring – the only gift they can afford. Again.

Two under my eyes from the office do and the small one of giblets left in the roasted turkey. Sackfuls of wrapping for recycling, another of unwanted gifts for Oxfam.

Bagsy a break.

13. A Few Kind Words

"Oh, here she is now," I said brightly. I smiled too, doing my best to convey pleasure at seeing Jeanette's face behind the group of other mothers I'd been chatting to at the school gate.

"Hello, Adelle," she said. She too was making an effort. Then, with more warmth, she greeted some of the others by name. Jeanette came a bit unstuck then, as it became clear she couldn't remember them all. Can't blame her really. My girls have always attended this school. Her boys only joined after the half-term break, just a couple of days ago.

Just before her floundering threatened to make everyone uncomfortable I interrupted with, "We were just talking about you, Jeanette. I've been telling everyone I knew you quite well before you moved away."

"Oh! All good, I hope." She gave a nervous titter.

If it had been anyone else I'd have felt a great deal of sympathy. As it was Jeanette, I simply said, "Of course. How could it be anything else?"

She couldn't say so, but I could tell from her face that Jeanette wasn't certain my remarks about her would have been kind. She had a reason for that – she was judging me by her own standards.

A lot of people, myself included, like a bit of a gossip. For most of us mums it's the one good thing about the endless committees, fundraising groups and school support activities we end up getting involved in. The only way to escape is to get someone to replace you. They're pretty tedious, except for the gossipy chats as we wait to get started. I've made some good friends through those. We express concern for other people's misfortunes, share their good news, and generally have a laugh. Jeanette talks about people too, but it's not all harmless gossip.

When we'd been pupils at this school she'd tattled on me. "Adelle's taken the book I was reading!" or "Adelle won't let me have any crayons!"

To be fair that may have been true. Aged five I wasn't any better at sharing or considering other people's wishes than most other small children. In secondary school we began growing out of that kind of thing. Jeanette's attitude towards me changed too – it got worse. Maybe I'd accidentally done something to hurt her, but I couldn't think what. I tried asking, attempted to make friends. She wouldn't talk to me – just about me. She started all sorts of rumours, none of them kind. Most were just ridiculous. Nobody was going to believe shy little me was pregnant at thirteen, even if she hadn't claimed I was expecting triplets, each with a different father.

Her rumours became more believable. I lost my first serious boyfriend because she spread it about that I'd cheated on him. There wasn't a word of truth in it, but he believed what he heard and dumped me abruptly, harshly and in public. It was the worst thing that had ever happened to me and at the time I'd thought it was the worst thing which ever could. I cried for a week. At least.

I'd always kept out of Jeanette's way as much as possible, and made even more effort to do so after that. When I left school I'd thought my problems were over, and they were for a while. Then she started working for the same company as me. It was a good job and there weren't many of those about locally so I couldn't give it up just because she'd joined the firm.

I could easily have gossiped about her – told the bloke she fancied that the cake she'd made for his birthday was shop bought, or pointed out to the boss that Jeanette only started taking her elderly neighbour shopping after she'd discovered she was his aunt. I didn't though. Partly because I didn't want to be dragged down to her level, but also because I knew the consequences of such actions. Knew the pain they could cause.

She'd been there six months when I missed out on a promotion because she told people I was a drunk. Tears don't spill out of me at every setback, but I shed a few over that. I'd known I could do the job and was certain it would be mine. What really hurt though was apparently she'd been believed.

At school my friends had laughed about the daft claims she made. "Adelle stole a lipstick on Saturday," or "Adelle snogged three boys at Mira's party," or "Adelle says you're ugly." They knew it wasn't true, not because they'd been with me at the time, but because they knew what I was like.

The boy I'd been dating for eight months, and who I thought I'd loved, didn't have any reason to doubt my loyalty until he heard her spiteful remarks. Once he did he had no doubts at all – that she was telling the truth. I eventually realised there could be no love without trust and I was better off without him, but it took time.

Jeanette's accusations I was a drunk weren't entirely without foundation. I did arrive at work with a hangover, but only once. I'd got engaged the night before. I suppose it's just possible she really thought I had a secret problem. Maybe it was coincidence she waited to warn the boss about it until the afternoon I'd used my lunch break to buy supplies for the engagement party.

"Is there anything you'd like to talk about?" he asked as I was stuffing my locker full of bottles.

What I should have done was remind him of my engagement and invite him to the party, but I caught sight of Jeanette's smirking face and accused her of a lifetime's vendetta. I was angry and probably exaggerated. The incident persuaded the boss I wasn't quite ready for more responsibility. I worked hard to prove I was and I gained promotion at the next opportunity, becoming Jeanette's manager. She moved away soon after. I don't know if the two things were connected. My life after that was pretty much trouble free.

Then she came back. Of course I wasn't happy to see her, but I was polite, determined to be the better person. When I discovered she had children the same age as mine I got them all together so her boys would see a few friendly faces when they started school. My girls are little darlings, willing to be friends with anyone and I figured any offspring of Jeanette's would need all the help they could get. I told Jeanette about the Cub Scout group my girls went to, and where the best supermarket is and which day to put the bins out.

She never apologised for her earlier behaviour and I never openly referred to it, but I'm sure she sometimes felt the shadow of it ready to fall on her. What she didn't know, until that very moment at the school gate, was that I'd started talking about her.

"Oh yes, Jeanette. I've been saying good things about you," I said. My smile was surely broad and convincing by then. "I've said what a good baker you are, and how efficiently you organise things, how kind you are to elderly people and how community spirited you are. Things like that."

"Oh!" she said and tittered again.

As she did, I realised my words had all been true. I'd thought her actions cynical, but they can't all have been. True she'd taken our former bosses aunt shopping after learning her identity, but she'd found out because she visited her neighbours, talked to them, offered help. When she'd seen how being given a cake brought a smile to people's faces she'd learned to bake and colleagues who were feeling down often found a plate of cookies on their desk, or a little box of cupcakes marked with their name in the fridge.

Even the gossip which had hurt me, sometimes helped others. A girl at school was saved from making a bad mistake with an older man, a colleague got help with their gambling problem. I still don't think everything she said about me was intended to be helpful, but now I see they were small unkind acts by a usually kind person. They were mistakes, made when she was young. No doubt I'd made some myself.

"Is it true, Adelle?" I was asked. "Is Jeanette really the marvel you've made her out to be?"

"All that and more," I responded with a smile.

As Jeanette mouthed a silent thank you, I realised I'd waxed so lyrical it was clear to all the other mothers she'd be a real asset to every school, community and Scouts committee, fundraising team and support group going.

"Jeanette, how about bringing your kids round to mine?" I asked, allowing her to escape before she got badgered into joining them, and relieving others of their responsibilities.

I'm going to warn her how much time they take up, and how hard it is to get out of them once you join. I'm also going to suggest she does join the Scout group committee. Not to take my place, but to work alongside me. After all, the chats before meetings are a great way to make friends.

14. Family Planning

Ella stood in the hallway, studying her reflection. She wore bright blue stripey leggings, a short pink skirt and flowery blouse which contained, amongst other colours, the same yellow as the laces of her boots. The whole combination at once was quite an eyeful, but I rather like the bright, quirky style both my girls have made their own.

Just under an hour ago she'd come home in her uniform looking every inch the schoolgirl, then changed into someone completely different. It wasn't just her clothes…

Ella was sideways on, with her hand low on her belly, as though imagining a baby bump.

"Ella, what are you doing, love?" I chuckled. "You'll have me thinking I'm going to be a gran."

"Mum, I… " She spun to face me, her face flushing red.

"It's not true!" But I could see from her face it was.

The shock hit me. It wasn't just that she's barely sixteen, but that this was my sensible little Ella. I wanted to yell at her for being so foolish, tell her I loved her and would support her through what was to come, but no words came.

"I'm sorry … We were going to tell you together, this evening, and explain." She said it as though breaking the news gently would have made everything fine.

She stepped toward me, putting her hand on my arm. "It'll be OK, Mum," she said.

They were the words I should be saying to her, but I wasn't sure I believed them. We'd get through this somehow, I knew. She had difficult decisions to make. Whatever she decided would impact on the rest of her life and no option would be easy.

Her phone rang and she chatted cheerfully with a schoolfriend. How could she be so calm?

I was disappointed, but that didn't stop me loving my daughter and wanting to help. Somehow I had to show that.

How could Ella, who was always so responsible, always thought ahead, have got into this mess? Unlike her sister, she didn't do rash and impulsive. The Christmas before last Lauren, two years older, twice the trouble, wanted a puppy.

"They're so cute." She proved the point with photos.

It was a particularly expensive breed. The choice of a celebrity she admired. It being on the small side meant I might just have been able to afford to feed the thing, but no way could I buy it, or meet vets bills or anything else.

It was Ella who'd dragged Lauren down the rescue shelter. Not to look for a cheaper alternative, but so Lauren could prove what a responsible dog owner she'd make. They went every day after school, to walk dogs and clean out kennels. Lauren went off the whole idea after an hour of picking up poop and walking in the rain. Ella insisted they stick it out until the end of the month, because they said they would and she didn't want to let them down. Although I know Ella's heart went out to the animals she saw, no kind of pet was ever suggested after that.

Did she seriously think a baby would be any easier to care for? And what about school? Ella's always been hardworking and clever. Lauren is retaking exams this year, but I'm expecting Ella to get much better grades the first time round. I was.

It was Ella who insisted the TV be off as she did her homework spread over the table. Knowing she couldn't eat or watch a show until Ella had done hers, meant Lauren usually managed to hand something in. I'd always thought Ella was the sensible one, the good influence. Even the vibrant clothes my girls wear are down to her. When Lauren nagged for the latest fashions, Ella said rather than follow trends, she should set them. That meant avoiding high street stores and going to charity shops and rummage sales.

Have I made Lauren sound irresponsible? She isn't really, not all the time anyway and she's constantly learning from her little sister. Sometimes it feels as though Ella has had as much to do with raising Lauren as I have. If anyone could cope with a teenage pregnancy, it was her. Especially if she didn't have to do it alone.

When she ended the call, I told her she had my support. "It won't be easy, love, but we'll manage."

"Of course we will, Mum." Immediately she was coming up with plans. We'd begin looking for bargain cribs and buggies. Exams would be over before the baby arrived, so she and Lauren could get jobs with different hours and share baby care. We'd take it in turns to have the baby with us at night, so we could sleep through twice as often as not.

I was worried her optimism the tasks could be split three ways was misplaced. "I'm sure your sister will want to help," I said. "But… " Actually there wasn't a but. Not so long ago Lauren, who's fond of children, would have offered but been unreliable. Recently she's matured. Given Ella's news, it could be said she'd overtaken her sister.

My thoughts were interrupted by the door opening. It was Lauren and she looked nervous.

We. That's what Ella said. We were going to tell you. That's when I realised. I would soon be a gran, but Ella wasn't going to be a mother just yet. Instead she'd be an aunt.

"Come here, love. It's all going to be OK," I told Lauren. And I knew, that between the three of us, we'd make that true.

15. Lucky To Be Alive

The High Street feels sticky. I'm not just referring to the tarmac melting underfoot, although that's happening on some roads. The air seems thicker somehow and people appear to be wading through it as though the heat has melted away their energy and enthusiasm. They're slumped sweating around the fountain, on benches, even on the ground. Everywhere I look, people seem hot and can't be bothered. I fit right in.

Something sparkly catches my attention as I pass Luigi's on the opposite side of the road. Was that tinsel? I stop and glance back. The Italian restaurant, which yesterday had tables outside, now has nothing on the wide pavement but two trees in pots marking the entrance. There's no sign of any tinsel. Of course not, it's July and I should know by now that it takes a lot more than wishful thinking to make everything right.

After the accident the doctors had said, "You're lucky to be alive, Mark."

I didn't believe it, but when I was shown the state of my crash helmet I saw what they meant; it was incredible I hadn't been killed. I was unconscious for… a few days I think. There are things from around that time I still can't properly remember.

They, the doctors and my family, said I'd recover and be able to do almost everything I could before. I didn't believe that either. Why would I when I could see for myself it wasn't true? No amount of bandaging and hospital sheets could hide the fact that one leg was considerably shorter than the other and lacked a foot.

When my girlfriend of the time finished with me I said it was for the best and that I didn't blame her. That was true. We'd not been that serious, chances are it wouldn't have worked out anyway. I wouldn't have wanted her to stay with me out of pity and I was giving her no other reason to stick around.

"We can still be friends," she said.

I didn't believe that. No one ever believes that. Or if they do, it's not something they want to happen.

When my family said, as I couldn't be at home with them for Christmas, they'd bring it to me in hospital, I thought I didn't care. Actually I was glad they did. Not because of the tinsel and turkey but because it showed me how much I mattered to them. It made me determined to try to recover for their sakes.

When my brother gave me a pack of socks and bag of stick on googly eyes I was confused at first.

"To make puppets of course," he said as though I was still concussed. "Out of all the leftover right socks."

Some people were uncomfortable about that, but I laughed. Until then everyone had been so nice, polite and tactful. My brother teasing me was the most normal thing which had happened to me since my bike skidded on black ice and sent me into the path of a lorry going in the opposite direction.

"Idiot. Socks are the same for either foot," I told him.

"Idiot am I?" He stepped away from the hospital bed. "Come here and say that."

"One day, little brother. One day soon." I'm not sure if I meant that, but I did it anyway. Learned to walk I mean.

When people stared at my leg, Mum said they were just concerned about how I was getting on, or interested in my prosthesis. Since Johnny Peacock had danced on Strictly, having a prosthetic leg was almost cool she reckoned.

"There's nothing cool about Strictly, Mum I said." I did mean that. Still, there was no getting away from the fact that Johnny, who had exactly the same amount of legs as I did, could move far better than I'd done even before the crash. I didn't get myself any sequins, but I did get on with my life.

By the next Christmas I had a job and by Easter a car and licence to drive it. I was still living at home, but not because I couldn't cope on my own. It was rent or a mortgage I couldn't manage and that had very little to do with my injuries.

Some of my old friends drifted away, but that would probably have happened anyway. My brother stayed close and I was glad of that.

"Being with you makes me feel normal," I told him. "You're so odd anyone seems normal next to you." That second bit wasn't absolutely true, but I was beginning to feel I could have a normal life.

When Becky said she'd go out with me I almost didn't believe her. I almost hadn't asked her, but my brother said if I didn't after the way I'd been staring at her all evening she'd think I was a stalker and call the cops.

For the first date I took her to dinner. Somewhere I could park right outside, so she didn't know about the leg.

Then we went to the pictures. I didn't tell her then either.

I met her outside the toy shop her family owned and where she worked, and took her to lunch at Luigi's and she still didn't know. We had dinner together again and I didn't say a word. My brother and his girlfriend made up a foursome for drinks in a pub with a live band one evening. His cryptic hints went right over Becky's head.

I kissed her, but nothing more. She probably thought I was a gentleman rather than an amputee wondering how to drop that piece of information into the conversation. We'd tentatively talked about children, her job led to that conversation. We both liked them we said and hoped to have our own one day. She blushed. I should have done too, for shame that she didn't yet know that my kids were likely to have twice as many toes as their dad. I was also thinking they might have Becky's hair and cheeky grin.

I never did tell Becky about my leg. Mostly cowardice I suppose, but my confidence still wasn't what it had been before the crash and I wondered if it was worth putting us both through it if she was just going to dump me after a few weeks anyway.

Becky discovered the truth for herself when we shared an early evening picnic under the shade of a huge oak in the park and she spilled a little of her drink on my lower leg. As she tried to dab it away she got a bit of a shock. Of course she did.

"I'm sorry, I should have told you," I said.

"It's probably not something that's easy to drop casually into a conversation."

"No."

"Were you born with it? Without I mean?" she asked.

After that awkward question it all seemed OK. Even as I was driving her home and asked if I could see her again I thought it was all going to be OK.

"What do you have in mind?" she asked.

I wanted it to be something nice, to make up for letting her discover about my leg that way, so I didn't answer immediately. What would she like to do? What would be romantic and convince her my false foot needn't make any real difference? It wasn't until we were almost outside her house that I remembered a colleague had done a canal boat holiday and mentioned the company would sometimes hire them out for a day. Weekends in the middle of a July heatwave would be booked already, but we both work Saturdays anyway. Becky's family shop has half day closing on Thursdays, so I'd recently swapped my day off so we could be together then.

I imagined taking Becky through a couple of locks, just for fun and to prove my ability to jump on and off the boat. Then once the novelty wore off we could moor up somewhere and enjoy having a floating home to ourselves for a few hours.

"How about a boat trip on Thursday? Maybe you could get the morning off too. It'll be cooler on the water and..." I trailed off as I saw her shaking her head.

"Sorry, I can't," she said. "I'm going to a Christmas lunch."

"Christmas lunch?" I asked. "Yeah, of course you are." I didn't try to hide how insulted I felt by that ridiculous excuse.

From her expression it was clear she realised how unconvincing that sounded, but she didn't try to put it right. "I really am..."

"Just go," I told her. Yelled, probably. I didn't want to hear how sorry she was, or anything else intended to make her feel better about breaking my heart.

"Mark, please." She put her hand up, as though to touch my face and I slapped it away. Then she got out. Becky looked upset, but that didn't help.

I drove away. Not far away thankfully, or I might have been involved in another crash. I moved the car out of sight, stopped and sobbed. I might have cried from the pain of my accident or the shock of losing my leg. I don't remember. I hadn't cried in the eighteen months since. Not when I got dumped from my bedside. Not when I realised I'd never ride a motorbike again. Not when a young cousin saw my stump for the first time and screamed. Not when I'd staggered across a bar on my still very new leg and asked out a girl who'd said no in a phrase starting with one f and ending with two. Looking back, she'd probably assumed I was legless in a different way, but it really knocked my confidence for a while.

Losing Becky hurt so much more. It felt like I was losing everything. All hope of a normal future anyway. I'd have been devastated I suppose even if she'd dumped me for something unconnected with my leg, but knowing it was that hurt so much. I'd loved her and thought she loved me, but she couldn't even give me the truth or the courtesy of a plausible lie.

Eventually I went home and shut myself in my room with my headphones on full. It was something I'd done a lot when I first came out of hospital. My family had come to understand my occasional need to shut out the world for a while. My brother was away on a training course, but it wouldn't have made any difference. I wouldn't have let him in.

The next morning my phone was missing. I remembered Becky had called when I'd given in to self pity and cried. Rather than answering I'd switched it off and thrown it. No doubt it was in the car somewhere, but I didn't look for it. What if there was a message from Becky? What if there wasn't?

Somehow I got myself in to work. I doubt I did anything useful while I was there. At least I was surrounded by people who'd have stopped me doing anything stupid if I'd thought of trying that. I don't think I thought of anything at all. When I got home I retrieved my phone from the back seat. It showed I'd missed several calls from Becky and one from my brother. There were texts too, which I deleted unread.

Becky tried calling me again that evening. I didn't answer. What would she have said? That we could still be friends? I'd heard that one before.

My brother sent another text. *'Please speak to Becky. She wants to explain.'*

He'd keep trying, I knew. He'd keep trying to talk to me until he thought I was OK, so to shut him up, I replied. *'It's OK, I understand. It's all good.'*

His response was a smiley face.

That was yesterday.

I dragged myself out of bed and to work again today. My colleagues asked if I was OK and I said I was.

Later the boss called me into her office.

"What's wrong, Mark?" she asked.

I tried telling her it was nothing, but my mis-buttoned shirt and the fact I was there on my day off made that hard.

She went to fetch me a coffee. "Drink that and then perhaps you'd be kind enough to go and fetch me a newspaper?"

It was an odd request; she didn't generally treat me like an errand boy, so I supposed she thought a walk would make me feel better. I accepted the suggestion as an easier alternative than trying to say Becky's name without breaking down.

I wander listlessly up the hot, sticky High Street. As I pass Luigi's, something sparkly catches my attention. Or my wishful thinking imagination. I want to see shops and restaurants draped in tinsel and almost convince myself I can. I stop and glance back. The Italian restaurant which yesterday had tables outside now has nothing but two trees in pots on the pavement. Not those lollipop bay trees or anything else Mediterranean looking, but Norway spruce. The hot sun, glinting on the windows looks almost like there's a gold star on top of each of them. Unless… it might not just be reflected sunlight.

I cross the road for a proper look. They really are spruce trees with stars on top. I peer through a window. Inside, the staff are decorating tables with candles and holly sprigs. Draped around the room is a thick garland of tinsel. If I was right about that, then maybe I was wrong about everything else.

When my phone buzzes again I answer Becky's call.

"Go to Luigi's if you don't believe me," she says.

"Believe you about what?"

"The Christmas lunch." There's a pause. "You've not read my texts or spoken to your brother, have you?"

"No."

"Mark, please just don't hang up until I've explained, OK?"

"OK."

"As soon as I said it I realised it sounded like a rubbish excuse, and you must have thought I was giving you the brush off, but it really is our Christmas lunch today. December is the busiest time for toy shops, so we have it in the summer."

That did make sense. "I thought… "

"I know. I'm so sorry. At first I didn't realise why you were so angry, but you thought it was about your leg, didn't you?" She didn't give me a chance to confirm that. "It wasn't. That was a shock, but I'm sure I'll get used to it."

"So, you're having lunch at Luigi's?"

"Yes. Stupid thing is I'd wanted to invite you. I nearly did just after we met, but I thought it might seem pushy. It's mostly family and meeting the parents can be a big deal and I didn't know if you'd still want to be with me by now. Then it seemed too late, as though I'd only be asking as an afterthought, not because I wanted you there."

She'd doubted I'd want to be with her? My fault; I'm not good at sharing my emotions. "Oh, Becky."

"Yeah, I worry too much about how to say things. You too, I guess. There are things we should just say, aren't there?"

"Like that I've only got one leg?"

"I was thinking more of I love you and would you like to meet my family for Christmas lunch in an hour's time at Luigi's?"

"I'd like that very much and I love you too, Becky."

The High Street feels happy. I'm not just referring to the brightly coloured, loose fitting clothes and smiling, sun kissed faces, although they're everywhere I look. The air seems supportive somehow and people are relaxing in it as though the heat has melted away their worries. They are sitting, to chat and laugh, around the fountain, on benches, even on the ground. Everywhere I look, people seem joyful. I fit right in.

16. Mollie's Chance To Shine

Mountains of Christmas decorations greeted me at work. Their festive cheer at odds with my sadness. Although they'd invited me as usual, I wouldn't be foisting myself on my sister Thelma and her family. I'd still send presents, but wouldn't see them opened. A shame as I'd got the boys real crackers of gifts, if you'll pardon the pun.

They didn't need another setting at the overcrowded table or the bother of making me feel involved. Thelma always allowed me to preside over dessert. Each year I carried in the steaming pudding as everyone clapped and stamped their feet. The lights were turned out. Hush descended as I spooned over warmed brandy. Cheers erupted as blue and orange flames danced and spluttered.

"We might have gone slightly overboard, Cait," Bridget, our boss, interrupted my thoughts.

"Sorry?"

"The Christmas decorations. I wasn't expecting so much."

I raised my bag of tinsel. "Don't bother with mine then."

"Don't be daft. You made the effort to bring it, so we'll put it up."

We transformed the beige office into a technicolour riot. Bridget and I ensured nobody reached too far from the top of stepladders or tripped over heaps of shimmering foil. There were giggles and screeches as more and more strands were looped around the room. Throughout it all Mollie circulated, passing up drawing pins and sticky tape exactly when needed.

The result would have put any Santa's grotto to shame. As well as tinsel and streamers, baubles and paper chains, wreaths and cellophane snowflakes, furry reindeer and fluffy Santas, there were seven strands of lights.

"We should have a proper switching on ceremony," I said.

"Great idea. Bridget can make a speech."

A phone rang. Mollie ably dealt with the query before anyone else could locate their desk.

"I have a better idea," Bridget said. "Mollie will you do it?"

"Me?" she gasped. Her face glowed pink.

"Yes. Tomorrow morning at eleven."

Mollie is one of those people you notice more when she's absent than when she's present. We always have tea bags and fresh milk thanks to Mollie. If there's any kind of argument or hurt feelings she says the right thing to soothe ruffled feathers and restore good humour. She helped run things in Bridget's absence by quietly suggesting, "Bridget would probably do it this way."

Mollie hesitated then said, "Thank you. I'd like to."

I watched her smile grow wider throughout the day as people said they were looking forward to her speech or asked what she was going to wear. Clearly she intended to enjoy her moment of glory.

Mollie arrived the following morning clutching a holdall. She asked the two youngest girls, who heartily disliked each other, if they'd help her. Soon shrieks of laughter were heard from the ladies' locker room.

Mollie emerged, flanked by the girls. She looked like a fairy queen with two dazzling princesses in attendance. Between them they'd fashioned cloaks and sashes from what must once have been curtains. They'd created crowns from paper and lavish jewellery from the shiniest baubles and tinsel. They should all have looked dreadful but somehow the effect was magical. Maybe their smiles and sparkling eyes made the difference.

Mollie's speech was read from an impressive scroll and contained as much tongue in cheek pomp as we could have wished for. Clapping, cheers and stamping of feet followed. The 'event' ended with mince pies and Buck's Fizz all round, courtesy of Bridget.

When I got home that evening my brother-in-law was waiting. "What's all this about letting us down over Christmas? I thought we could rely on you, Cait," he said.

"Sweet of you to put it like that, Charles, but you'll do fine without me in the way."

"Don't be daft! Who'll stop the boys rowing, talk to Uncle Phil and deal with the pudding?"

"Thelma will cope perfectly."

"She loves concentrating on the food, knowing you and I are keeping everything relatively calm outside the kitchen and that the moment the turkey reaches the table she can relax and leave pudding to you. Besides, I once set light to a fancy dessert and lost my eyebrows so won't be risking that again. Mostly though, we'd really miss you."

Maybe they would. I remember when the office photocopier ran out of ink during Mollie's holiday. It wasn't until then we realised nobody else had a clue how to replace it. Tempers frayed and voices rose. On Mollie's return she got us all back on friendly terms.

Whether my family needed me or not wasn't the point though. They'd invited me because they wanted to and I should accept because that's what I wanted.

"Thank you, Charles. I'll be delighted to come and of course I'll bring a pudding." I wondered if I could find a chef's hat with a holly pattern to give the lighting ceremony an extra touch of festive cheer.

17. Walking The Dog

"Horace sit!"

He did; on Lynne's foot. Pleased with himself for being so obedient he wagged his tail and sniffed hopefully at the pocket containing meaty treats.

Lynne was cold, wet and muddy. She was all tangled up, in an extendable dog lead and bits of bramble, with no hope of escape. The worst part was that it was entirely her own fault. She'd landed herself in this mess in an attempt to avoid being trapped in a different way.

She'd had a good job in a London marketing agency and was sharing a flat with Andrew. Although she'd not realised it, she'd been caught up in the rat race. Living close to the good job required a large rent. Her status meant she was expected to socialise at exclusive venues, paying for meals and drinks, plus clothes and shoes. She'd enjoyed it for a while.

Then her relationship with Andrew failed. They'd pooled their resources to lease the flat. Neither could afford the rent alone. If one of them could have left, they'd still have split up but would have remained civil. Working together wouldn't have been so awful either.

The one positive was that it helped Lynne see the truth. Although she'd been happy enough when she and Andrew were a team, Lynne didn't love her job and the stresses which came with it. The things her wages bought lost their shine without anyone to share them with. The flat no longer felt like home. Going out was no longer a pleasure, just better than staying in to argue with Andrew. He was a decent man whom she shouldn't hate.

"Think I'll stay with my parents for the long weekend," she told Andrew.

"Good idea… Give them my best."

During the train journey Lynne looked forward to relaxing and simply enjoy being with people she cared about. Since leaving home she'd kept in touch with her parents, but phone calls or rushed visits with Andrew weren't the same as sharing their company as she had when she was a child.

The first hour was bliss, the next two days were dreadful. Lynne's once loving parents constantly bickered over the TV.

"There's no escape from the football," Mum said.

"Those dreary soaps you mean," Dad snapped.

"Stop it you two! You sound just like me and Andrew," Lynne said.

She persuaded them into giving up watching TV for a couple of days in the hope that, just as she'd done, they'd see what was important; and she'd get the peace she craved.

It worked. With the television off they all chatted pleasantly on Sunday evening and on Monday they did some of the things she remembered from childhood. They all cooked pancakes, walked in the nearby woods, played board games and laughed a lot. Lynne returned to her flat and job in a better mood than she'd experienced for some time.

Lynne went back to her parents' home the next Friday. Both said they realised how much time they'd wasted either watching TV or arguing about it.

"Tell the truth, I'm glad to have missed United's last match. They lost three nil," Dad said. "And I didn't even bother checking the results of some of the games I'd normally have watched, which shows I'm not really that interested. Just got into the habit of watching."

"Same with me," Mum said. "When I looked in my magazine to see what I'd missed in the soaps, the terrible things I'd worried might happen to the characters hadn't. Instead it was something even worse! Seeing it written out like that made me realise it's all a bit depressing. I don't really enjoy watching, I'd just got used to it."

"We're considering getting another dog," Dad announced. "Going out with you the other day reminded us how much we like walking."

"The exercise will do us good," Mum added.

"That's a great idea!" Lynne said. She'd had a Yorkshire terrier from when she was eight until her early twenties. They'd all been heartbroken when Beverley didn't wake up one morning. "I can help with the walking and look after if it if you go away or anything."

"But you won't be here, love," Mum said.

"Actually... I was hoping I would be." She explained she and Andrew weren't just going through a rough patch, and how she felt trapped. "If I could stay here while I look for a job locally I could help out while the dog settles in."

"You won't get the same kind of job round here," Mum warned.

"That suits me perfectly."

They both assured her she was welcome back home for as long as she wanted to be there.

That weekend they visited a rescue kennels, looked at some totally adorable little balls of fluff and enquired about the adoption process. Afterwards Lynne returned to London to hand in her notice.

She had three weeks of finishing off work projects, saying goodbye to colleagues, visiting the letting agency, phone updates about the new dog and packing her belongings. At the end of it, Andrew had a potential new flatmate, her parents had Horace, and Lynne was temporarily unemployed, homeless and happy.

Horace was a surprise. She'd known he was almost adult and very cute. She guessed he wouldn't be another Yorkshire terrier, but not that he was seven stone of very hairy and even more boisterous Old English Sheepdog.

"The people who bought him as a puppy just couldn't cope," Dad explained.

"He's as good as gold," Mum said. "As long as he gets plenty of exercise and attention – and you did say you'd help."

Horace was a real softy and quite obedient if Lynne could keep him calm enough to listen to instructions. But if she lost concentration for two seconds he'd steal the ice cream from a passing child, slobber the evidence on her clothes and almost dislocate her shoulder as something else caught his interest and he dragged her through the nearest puddle. She did love him though and found it very therapeutic to wash and brush him.

Lynne's attempts at job hunting reminded her why she'd left for the city in the first place. There were companies with vacancies, jobs she liked the sound of, and managers willing to interview her, but never all three in one package. The local pub employed her three nights a week to wash glasses and help in the kitchen, which was a lot better than nothing.

The important thing was that she was no longer trapped, at least not until she took Horace across open countryside for a change. The footpath looked well used, but the only people she saw using it were a long way off.

Although she couldn't see any farm animals or other dogs, Lynne kept Horace on his long lead just in case. Now and again he tried to bolt off after rabbits, some of them imaginary. Once this sent her sprawling in wet grass, but she had him fairly well under control most of the time. He was really good at walking to heel until he forgot or was distracted. As long as he actually listened when she said it, he was excellent at sitting on command. Each time he followed her instruction, Lynne rewarded Horace with a meaty treat.

It wasn't a rabbit which sent him racing off into the patch of brambles, but a model plane. A plane which circled overhead, sending Horace racing round in circles. Circles which got smaller as the lead wrapped around Lynne, pinning her arms to her sides and drawing her ever more firmly into the bramble thicket just as it started to rain.

"Stop it," she yelled to plane, rain and dog. Only the weather paid any attention.

"Just stay still, will you?" That got the same lack of response from Horace.

"Horace sit!"

He did; on Lynne's foot. Pleased with himself for being so obedient he wagged his tail and sniffed hopefully at the pocket of meaty treats.

His seven stone weight wasn't a problem as Lynne's feet were fast sinking into the soft mud which produced a cushioning effect. The way he was slobbering over her didn't really matter either, as she was already muddy. The wagging tail was more of an issue as every swipe felt as though it could dislocate her knees. Even so, Lynne would give him a treat as soon as she could wriggle a hand free to get one.

Lynne tried shouting for help, without much hope. Whoever was flying the plane could be a long way off and probably the noise of the engine would drown out her calls. Just as it seemed as though she might be stuck until lack of food made her thin enough for her bindings to loosen, a voice called, "Do you need some help?"

If this had been one of Mum's soaps the rescuer would either steal Horace, turn out to be a twin separated at birth, or the owner of the plane who was working a drug racket and would force her to be his mule.

She was actually a total stranger who seemed very nice, although anyone with the power to rescue her would probably have seemed charming. Lynne introduced herself and Horace.

"Sit," she said just in time to prevent him adding his own greeting of welcome by slobbering on their rescuer.

"Hello, you," the woman said, making a fuss of Horace. "Oh sorry… and hello to you too, Lynne. I'm Elaine."

"Nice to meet you and yes, I would welcome some help. Any ideas?"

"I think we might have to let Horace off the lead to untangle you. Will he run off if I let go?"

"I'm not sure." Lynne explained about him being a rescue dog and not having been with her family long. "There's a short lead in my pocket if you can reach it."

Elaine extracted both the lead and the pack of treats. With those she had no trouble persuading Horace to stay close as she set about releasing Lynne. It was a little disconcerting to be manhandled by a woman she'd just met.

The same thought seemed to have occurred to Elaine. "This is cosy," she said as she teased a bramble stem from Lynne's hair. "I think we'd better decide right now that we're going to be good friends."

"Deal," Lynne said.

As Elaine prised the last thorny branch away and began unwinding the lead, Lynne chattered away about moving back in with her parents and her temporary job in the pub.

"I'll pop in and see you one night," Elaine said.

"Please do. I definitely owe you a drink. Sorry, you're getting horribly muddy."

"Oh don't worry about me, I'm used to it. You should be more worried about Horace. You're going to have fun cleaning him."

"Actually I will. He loves having a bath and I love cleaning him up and brushing his coat."

"Do you now? That's interesting."

"It is?"

"Yes. Not to me so much as my brother. He runs a dog grooming business and is looking for an assistant."

"And I'm looking for a job," Lynne said as at last she was released. It barely occurred to her that if Elaine's brother were single and had his sister's charming personality, lovely smile and chocolate coloured eyes she might be about to get herself entangled all over again.

18. One Man's Junk

"Gordon will you look at that!" Cindy said, pointing at the screen and ignoring the fact her husband was already watching The Antiques Roadshow. "It's just like yours."

"A bit, yes," he agreed.

"Exactly like it and it's right at the end of the programme, so maybe it's worth a bit? They usually keep the really valuable stuff until last."

"Hush up then, woman, and we'll find out."

The china plate was worth a bit; about ten pounds the ceramics expert guessed. It was a reproduction, though an old one of good quality. Had it been an original the owner would have been advised to insure it for at least £6,000.

"Six thousand, Gordon! We could have a holiday with that kind of money. A really swanky one."

"Yes, but not with ten pounds, or more likely five because mine has a chip."

"That just means it's more likely to be really old."

"Not really, Cindy love. You said it was exactly like the one on the telly. As that was a fake, I expect mine is too."

When the programme finished, Cindy made them both a mug of tea and cut a round of sandwiches. That gave her time to think. She worked out why Gordon wasn't very excited about owning a valuable antique. Silly fool had thrown it away. Gordon was always throwing things away.

She tackled him about it when she brought in their tea.

"Of course I've not. You don't ever let me throw anything away so we hoard all kinds of junk, just in case it might come in useful."

"Well, it might."

"If it did, we'd never find it. There's not room in that garage even for a flashlight to go looking, let alone one of us, and as for the car ..."

"All right, I admit it is a bit untidy. I'll help you clear it up tomorrow and we can look for that plate at the same time."

"If you like, but it won't be an easy job."

The next morning, after a breakfast of scrambled eggs on toast and two mugs of tea to fortify themselves for the task ahead, Gordon opened the garage door. "After you, love."

It took Cindy twenty minutes to move enough junk to reach the light switch.

"OK, I get your point. Some of this stuff will have to go," Cindy said, dragging out a bag of newspapers she'd kept because she hadn't had time to finish the crosswords.

They discovered boxes from things they no longer owned, their old frame tent still in good condition, two cans of woodstain that would be useful to tart up the fence as well as off cuts of lino from the bathroom.

She wished she'd remembered they were there when she'd spilled the hair dye. If she had they could have replaced the piece which got stained instead of taking it all up and putting in a carpet. Although Cindy didn't say so, she started to see George's point about the saved items never actually coming in handy. Well nearly everything; those old knitting needles could be used to mark rows of seeds in the garden... although then she supposed they should get rid of the bundle of lilac prunings she'd saved to do that same job.

They set aside the things to keep and filled the back of the car with junk.

"Shall I take this lot down the tip, while you sort out a bit of lunch?" Gordon asked.

"OK." Cindy hated the tip; all those useful odds and ends, plus decent furniture, going into landfill seemed such a waste. She did start to see that a bit of space in the garage would be a good thing though. It would be nice to just walk to the freezer without climbing over stuff and banging her shins.

After lunch they filled the car again and twice more on Tuesday. Cindy was growing more determined to find the plate; after all the work they were doing they really needed that holiday. She'd like a few days by the sea to blow the cobwebs away. Not the Caribbean, that would be too hot and she didn't fancy spending all day on the plane getting there. France perhaps, that wasn't too far, and she'd found a phrase book a few minutes ago. What had Gordon done with that?

"It's here," he said, pointing to the 'keep' pile, when she asked.

They soon discovered a third category; things Cindy admitted they'd probably never use and George conceded were too good to chuck out.

"We could give them to a charity shop," he suggested.

"Oh no!" Cindy wailed. "I've just remembered what happened to the plate."

"You don't mean to say you gave it to Oxfam?"

"Yes, sorry, but it was your fault."

"Mine how?" Gordon asked.

"After you took my old athletics trophy to the tip, I thought you'd throw everything out, so I …"

She trailed off as George produced her trophy.

"You don't think I'd chuck away something like that? I just took some rubbish to the tip in order to put in a cupboard for things worth keeping."

She hugged him. "I do love you and I'm so sorry about your plate and our holiday."

"Well, we've still got the tent. Fancy a week camping?"

She thought for a moment and decided she did. "Yeah, that'd bring back some memories."

"Pity we got rid of the sleeping bags and gas stove," Gordon said.

"Actually, we didn't. I put them in the attic." Not just them either. She'd better book two weeks at the campsite, they'd need it once they'd cleared the attic.

19. Careful What You Wish For

"Here's your present, Love." Marcus handed Annie a tiny, beautifully wrapped box. "I'm almost sure it's exactly what you want."

As she reached to take the gift from him Annie felt a twinge in her cracked ribs and plastered arm, reminding her what happened the last time she got what she'd wished for. Things would be different this time she assured herself, in fact they already were.

Last Christmas Marcus had given her a cookbook. Marcus, a loving husband and talented musician, wasn't good at buying presents nor, until recently, most other everyday tasks. He'd always had an excuse of sorts though.

Last year, as she'd stirred the Christmas pudding, Annie had made a wish; that Marcus would do just one of the household chores, so she didn't feel she must do everything herself. And without her having to explain and remind him so many times it would have been easier if she'd just done it anyway. Until ten days ago it hadn't come true. She'd come home from work to find Marcus practising a new song on his guitar. He hadn't washed up his plate and fork after eating the lunch she'd prepared and left in the fridge.

"I'm leaving them to soak," he'd said.

"Could you unload the food from the car, please? I did the shopping on the way home. I'll weed the front garden before I cook dinner."

"Oh, the garden…" Marcus mumbled. "I did try but wasn't sure which were the plants and which were weeds. I didn't want to pull up the wrong thing."

Annie saw him fetch in the shopping while she was in the garden. He even returned the reusable carrier bags to the boot. After she'd finished the weeding she found everything but the frozen items and the milk on the work surfaces.

Marcus shrugged. "I didn't know where you wanted it all."

"Have you started making dinner, then?" she'd asked.

"I thought you wanted to. Anyway, I don't know what we're having."

He had a point, which only made her more irritated. Rather than say something she might regret, Annie stomped off to tackle the torn stair carpet. She'd asked Marcus to look at it the previous week, but as usual he had an excuse.

"We should get a new one, but I don't know what pattern you'd like."

Annie tried to rip away the worst bit, but found she was holding nothing as she jerked her arm. She took a step to steady herself, and hurtled down, realising Marcus had eventually done one household task; tacking down the ripped section.

She'd ended up in hospital ten days before Christmas, with a broken arm, three cracked ribs and possible concussion, and a definite feeling she should have been far more careful what she'd wished for.

Marcus had at least been practical enough to call an ambulance. Once it was obvious she'd be staying overnight, he brought her cleansing lotion but no cotton wool, three black bras, one pair of knickers, a loose skirt that would be easy to put on and sheer top that wouldn't. He'd tried though and included the book she'd been reading and a pack of her favourite mints.

"What about the Christmas shopping?" he asked once he'd been assured she would suffer no long term problems and was reasonably comfortable.

"I've done most of it already. There's just the fresh food and a few presents that you'll have to get."

Annie had indeed bought most of the presents; all the easy ones. Every year Marcus expected her to choose gifts for their niece and nephew and his mother. Every year it got harder to find something suitable. This time he'd be the one dashing from shop to overcrowded shop.

He'd have to buy his own present too. Every year Annie tried so hard to get Marcus something he'd really like. She spent hours trying to find the perfect gift and almost always got it wrong. Often she'd tactfully suggest something to see if he was interested, bought and wrapped the gift that made his eyes light up when mentioned, then learned their conversation had encouraged him to go and buy the thing for himself three days before Christmas.

Every year, until last year, Marcus couldn't decide what she'd like and gave her money.

"You should have dropped hints," he said seeing her disappointment.

Last year he'd given her saucepans. She didn't blame him for that as she'd asked for them. She'd guessed any hints might be too subtle, so told him exactly what she wanted.

"I'd like some decent saucepans and something small as a surprise."

He'd bought the very best saucepans he could find and the cookbook. She did have to admit it was a surprise – she'd thought Marcus might have noticed they already owned that edition and that she used it on a regular basis. Or to be fair, maybe he had and saw it was starting to fall apart?

This year she'd not asked outright for her present but dropped hints just as he'd asked. She'd not been subtle at all. Surely even Marcus would realise she wanted a dishwasher?

"I can buy food if the list says exactly what to get but I'm not sure about the presents," he said.

"I can't shop with a broken arm. I can't drive or carry much."

"I'll do the driving and carrying."

Yes, while she got bashed about by the crowds and still had all the worrying to do.

"Besides, I don't know what to get," he'd said, just as he did every year.

"Shouldn't be too hard," she echoed his previous reply when she'd made that same complaint. "Your mum likes gardening, young Tom likes music, Suzie loves reading."

"Right, I'll see what I can do," he said miserably.

She reached out to squeeze his hand and offer help but the movement jolted her ribs and made her head swim. She was already suffering the pain of a wish come true, so just for once she was really going to make sure she got what she wanted.

"Marcus, I'd really like a present this year instead of money. I feel I'm missing out on the build up to Christmas as I'm not wrapping presents or writing cards or putting up the decorations."

She knew he didn't think she was missing much by leaving these tasks to him, but at least he couldn't use the excuse she hadn't made her wish clear.

Annie had been home for a week when Marcus announced he'd done all the gift shopping. "I got a garden centre voucher for Mum, book token for Suzie and an i-tunes credit for Tom."

She shook her head; why hadn't she thought of doing that? They could all get exactly what they wanted but would still know some thought had gone into the gift.

"Got yours too, but I'll keep it as a surprise for Christmas Day."

"Lovely". There was something else small in his bag. She guessed it was another pack of her favourite mints that he'd wrap for her to open on the day. Hopefully he'd ordered the dishwasher for delivery soon after Christmas.

She started to feel mean about her unkind thoughts about him when she'd been in hospital. He'd been wonderful since she'd come home. He'd done a brilliant job of decorating the tree and had cooked every meal, although she did have to stand and watch, giving constant instructions. Fortunately he soon got the hang of washing up, so Annie could relax after she'd eaten.

On Christmas Day Marcus produced a simple version of the traditional feast then cleared everything away. He was delighted with the cheque she gave him to get his own gift.

"Thanks, love. I knew you wouldn't be able to shop for me so I've picked out what I'd like and this is more than enough to cover it." Then he handed her a package and told her it was exactly what she'd wished for.

"Do you remember what you said?" he asked.

She looked at the small parcel he held. "I mentioned washing up was impossible with a broken arm and I didn't fancy going back to it once the cast was off."

He looked startled. "Oh, I didn't realise that was the hint."

"Why did you think I kept mentioning it then?"

Marcus gave his characteristic shrug. "Didn't really think about it. Look, I know it's not exactly a present but I'm quite happy to do all the washing up in future. I know where everything goes now and know what to do; I just get off all the food then dry everything so it's nice and shiny."

"Wow." She'd wanted Marcus to do just one practical task in the home and now he would. She didn't need a gift now, which was just as well as he clearly hadn't ordered her dishwasher. Even so, he had given her a gift and whatever it was it would be a surprise.

"So what did you think was a hint?" Annie asked as she clumsily pulled away the ribbon and unfolded the wrapping which was mercifully free of sticky tape.

"You wanted your hands to look nice and have something sparkly to hand every day."

"Yes, that was a hint," she admitted. Annie opened the box to reveal a gorgeous diamond ring. "And this is exactly what I wanted. Thanks, love."

20. Best Man's Speech

When the doorbell rang, Jo assumed it was her friend, and soon to be bridesmaid, returning because she'd forgotten something. Even so, she checked through the spy hole first. Good thing she did.

Instead of Gloria in the hallway it was Dave – the man who in a few days would be best man at her wedding. If she'd opened the door to him, expecting to see her friend, she'd quite likely have said something which could as interpreted as rude. Being polite to him was important, now more so than ever.

As Jo forced a smile, a worrying thought struck her. What was Dave doing here? Was there a snag about the wedding? Had something happened to Cameron? She felt suddenly cold as she pulled the door open.

"Don't panic, it's just about my speech," Dave said.

"Your speech?" Her smile became more natural with the relief it wasn't bad news.

"Yes, I thought you'd be w… What I mean is, I thought perhaps you'd like to see it?"

Had he been going to say she'd be worried? It sounded like that. She wasn't worried exactly. She'd already decided to laugh at whatever silly jokes he'd included, try not to get annoyed at him micromanaging the whole event, smile and sip her wine as he made toasts. It would all be fine.

"Oh, right. Come in."

He was right that she'd like to see it. That would help her prepare and give a good impression of being perfectly happy he was an important part of what, Dave or no Dave, was going to be the happiest day of her life. It was thoughtful of him to offer and kind to have made the journey. Dave was thoughtful and kind – she must remember that.

"What can I get you? Tea, coffee, a cold drink?"

"Tea would be great, thanks."

Jo pointed him towards the lounge. "Make yourself comfortable, or admire my sea view if you like. You're tall enough to catch a glimpse of it!" She hoped that sounded genuinely friendly.

In the kitchen Jo made tea and tried to make her feelings about Dave positive. She'd been dismayed when her beloved Cameron first introduced them, and too surprised to hide it. Looking at Dave's face, she'd known the feeling was mutual.

"You know each other," Cameron immediately realised. "Oh dear, you didn't go out together did you? That could be awkward."

"No, we didn't," Dave said with feeling at exactly at the same time Jo insisted, "It was nothing like that!"

Dave broke the short silence by explaining, "We once worked together."

"OK, so why those faces?" Cameron asked.

Jo's honest response would have been, 'because I don't like him and now it looks as though I'm going to have to spend the rest of my life pretending I do,' so she didn't say anything.

"It's rather a surprise to discover the person you've been looking forward to meeting for months is someone you already know," Dave said. "Perhaps I should have guessed. Jo is quite a common name though and I'd not seen her for a while even before I got the job in New Zealand."

It was a good answer. Maybe it was true? Jo had been looking forward to meeting her fiancé's best friend after all

Cameron had told her about their shared childhood. He'd sounded so nice.

"I really missed him when he first moved away," Dave had said. "Of course meeting you about then more than made up for his absence, but I'm really glad he's back for good."

When he'd told her that, Jo had been pleased too, but the Dave he'd described didn't tally with the man she remembered. Jo had found him irritating. He could be very silly and tended to sweat the small stuff. He was often pedantic, wanting every little detail to be exactly right. He'd sometimes made work plans very like hers. They weren't close enough for her to embrace wholeheartedly, and not quite different enough to object to without seeming petty. If she'd been able to have an occasional grumble about him she'd almost certainly have said very little and instantly forgotten whatever had annoyed her. The trouble was that everyone else liked him, so she felt she had to pretend she did too. That meant her mild irritation had escalated into resentment and dislike.

"Cameron told me you were in the Scouts together," Jo had said, hoping that would lead them to reminisce and allow her to see Dave as Cameron's old friend, not her annoying ex colleague. That tactic worked remarkably well. As the men had talked, their respect and affection for each other was clear. Jo was reassured that however little she liked Dave, he was a good friend to Cameron.

Jo did her best to get along with him for the sake of her fiancé, and felt certain Dave was doing the same. She tried to concentrate on his good points. She'd already known he was hard working and was generally efficient, unless he was butting heads with her. He was good looking and could be charming. She discovered he had plenty more positive attributes. He was amusing, provided you weren't trying to be serious. He was generous, with time and money. Now they weren't working together she disliked him less than had previously been the case.

Actually liking him was beyond her though. A lot of that was because she felt she had to like her fiancé's best friend, and be seen to. If she genuinely did like him she'd probably have been able to say when he slightly annoyed her and they'd have sorted it out, not left something constantly aggravating her like a sharp piece of grit in her shoe. As it was, she just pretended everything was fine.

Jo's act seemed to have fooled most people, even her friend Gloria, who'd met him at a couple of social events and the wedding rehearsal.

When she'd visited earlier that day she'd said, "I'm looking forward to the last of my bridesmaid duties."

"Doing something terrible to our car?" Jo guessed. She and Cameron had suspected Dave would have plans in that direction – just one reason they'd booked a taxi to collect them after the reception.

"As if I would! No, I mean dancing with the best man and well, making sure he's not lonely once you've gone off with his friend."

"You actually want to?" Jo asked.

"Any reason I shouldn't?"

"No. Nothing in particular." It was no good, she was going to have to tell someone. Keeping it bottled up was making things worse. "It's just that I don't like him."

"I know you didn't when you both worked at Jackson's but that was a long time ago. I thought you got on fine now?"

"I have tried. Oh ignore me, it's probably just pre-wedding nerves. I can see he's a nice person… "

"But?"

"Cameron likes him so much I feel I have to pretend I do too. And that makes me feel like I'm living a lie."

"You're massively overthinking this," Gloria said.

"I know and just telling you I don't like him is helping."

"Come on then, what's wrong with him?"

As Jo tried to explain she was interrupted by Gloria laughing.

"Oh, Jo! How many packs of paper napkins did you buy to compare with the lace trim on your dress to be sure it matched exactly?"

"What? I don't know, but those little details are important to bring the whole thing together."

"Right, and that stunt with your page boys at the rehearsal?" Gloria demanded.

"Hah! Their faces were a picture, weren't they? I wasn't just teasing them for no reason though. Everything had got so serious and people were on edge. Something was needed to lighten the mood."

"I wonder why Dave was so concerned to know how many cars the main wedding party would be using and exactly how big the church's car park is?"

"Didn't he go on about it? But yes, he was right to. If everyone parked there the car bringing me would have nowhere to stop to let me out, let alone for photos."

"And why do you think he used to make silly jokes in tense meetings?"

"Because he's always making silly jokes? And sometimes because they can help."

"He's very much like you in a lot of ways. That's the problem. He reminds you of your own very few, and very minor, failings and modesty blinds you to his better points."

After Gloria left, Jo had been mulling that idea over. As she did, the doorbell had sounded and she'd looked through the spy glass to see Dave in the hallway outside her flat.

Now she took tea into the lounge for them both. "Sorry I don't have any biscuits. I want to make sure I fit in the dress."

"I'm sure you will." He handed her a couple of sheets of paper.

Jo read through the speech. As she'd guessed there were some silly jokes and mildly embarrassing anecdotes about Cameron's youth. Of course there were – it wouldn't be a best man's speech without them. Including them wasn't Dave being annoying and silly, it was Dave getting it right.

There was a bit about Dave having met Jo first and having to go to the other side of the planet to get away from her. There was no truth in that, she'd left the company before that happened and it was clearly just another little joke. She turned the page.

"That bit about New Zealand... " Dave said. "Obviously it's not exactly accurate."

Jo read the next line, implying he'd forced himself into exile through despair he'd never be as lucky as Cameron. "No, I see that."

"Thing is, people know we worked together. I feel I need to say something."

"It's fine," she said. The joke was on him, not her and he was right that he could hardly not mention her at all.

Other than the toasts there wasn't much more to Dave's speech. Just a few lines saying how happy he was that his best friend had found the perfect woman for him.

"In case you're wondering, that bit is true, Jo. I really do think you're the perfect wife for Cameron and will make him happy – and I like you for that."

"But you don't actually like me?" she asked.

"I didn't. I think we both annoyed each other at work?"

Jo nodded agreement.

"And when I first realised you were Cameron's fiancée I was surprised and a bit concerned. Not now though. I've made an effort to be on friendly terms with you, just as I'm sure you've been doing. That's allowed me to see your good points and I think I would like you now, except… "

Jo remembered what her friend Gloria had said about the two of them being so similar. "You feel you have to?"

"Yes, I suppose that's it," Dave said.

"You think you should like me and must always act as though you do. But you don't, not with me."

"Really?"

"Yes, really. Come on, we'll admit how much we dislike each other, have a moan about the other's faults and get it off our chests."

"Ladies first," Dave said.

Jo knew both that she could tell him and that she didn't want to. Her moan to Gloria had made her see that his faults weren't big or numerous and that they did indeed mirror her own. Now she was at last free to dislike Dave she discovered she didn't.

"Come on, you must have something," he coaxed.

"OK, you worried me by turning up here. I thought something bad had happened."

"I'm sorry."

"Don't be. Your very first words were to reassure me that wasn't the case. That was kind and thoughtful of you. Much kinder than I've been to you. Right, your turn."

"All that time you spent fussing over napkins – and they're still not right!"

"What!"

He grinned. "Got you! They're perfect. Just as your wedding will be."

Jo knew he was right. With Dave organising things nothing would be allowed to spoil the day. Then she and Cameron would drive away in a nice plain, not decorated, not booby trapped, taxi. As she remembered Gloria's plan to keep Dave happy after that, Jo grinned. Perhaps she'd return from honeymoon to find that her best friend and her husband's best friend had become a couple.

21. Hunting Unicorns

Misha went up to say goodnight to her daughter.

Her brother's voice drifted out. "… and she and the unicorns lived happily ever after," Tim said.

"Will you take me to see a unicorn, Uncle Tim? Pleeeeease."

"We could go to the New Forest on Saturday and look, if Mummy says it's OK."

Misha wanted to push open the door and declare, "There's no such thing as unicorns!" Even without the issue of looking for imaginary creatures Misha would have to say no. The forest would be full of families, with children running about, having fun. Louise would have to watch from the car, unless the car park was smooth enough for her wheelchair to get her a little closer to the action she couldn't join.

Misha plastered on a smile, went in and kissed Louise.

"Mummy, can me and Uncle Tim go and look for unicorns on Saturday?"

"I'll think about it."

"Please, Mummy. Please, please."

"Good night, love."

Misha kissed her daughter again and tried to pretend she hadn't heard Tim whisper, "I'll talk to her, sweetie."

"No, Tim," she said as soon as they were back in the lounge. "I don't want Louise to see how much she's missing out on."

"She's missing even more by staying at home all weekend," Tim said.

Misha ignored that. "And please stop telling her those ridiculous fairytales. They just lead to disappointment."

They had for Misha. She grew up thinking the good guys always won and life was fair. When her prince told her they'd live happily ever after she'd believed him. Then, on the way home from a toddler's birthday party, another vehicle crashed into them. Louise, wearing her fairy costume, complete with sparkling wings and magic wand had been injured. Her father hadn't survived. That day Misha stopped believing in fairytales.

According to her brother it was also the day she stopped believing in fun, hope and happiness.

"Louise deserves those things and so do you," he'd said more than once. He tried to say it again.

"She's my daughter, Tim. I know you love her, but she's my responsibility and I make the rules."

"And it's a rule she can't have fun or make friends?"

"No, of course not. I want her to have friends, but I can't very well invite little girls back here after school when I'm at work can I? I've promised she can join the Brownies as soon as she's old enough and I've been meaning to do something one weekend. I could hire a film and get in popcorn. What do you think?"

"It's a good plan, as long as you let Louise have a share of the popcorn."

"I know you think I'm too strict about sweets, but sitting in that chair all day means she doesn't eat much so it needs to be good quality and..."

Tim raised his hands as though in surrender. "I know, Sis. You're trying to protect her. I do think you're trying a little too hard, but you're doing it for the right reasons. I'll respect your wishes in that, but if you want me to spend time with her, then I'm going to tell her fairytales."

"That's blackmail!"

Tim's shifts allowed him to pick Louise up from school and look after her until Misha finished work. Without his help, she couldn't keep her job and without her wages, Louise's quality of life would be even poorer.

"Maybe it is," Tim agreed, "but I'm sticking to it. If you're so concerned with her hearing only the truth, you'd better start telling it yourself."

"I do! You know I do!"

"Oh really? That 'I'll think about it' when she asked about going to the New Forest on Saturday. You'd already decided she couldn't go before she finished asking, hadn't you?"

She had of course.

"And the birthday party next week? You said you'd think about that too. If you did it was only about what could go wrong, not about how much fun she might have, or how much she wants to go. How much she hates you excluding her from so many of the fun things in life."

Misha gasped. Surely Tim could understand why she couldn't let Louise go to the homes of other children – especially not for birthday parties. And this wasn't going to be any ordinary party. It was being held at a farm and all the other little girls and boys would be feeding lambs, milking a goat and having pony rides. Louise probably wouldn't even be able to get her chair close enough to watch the fun and if she tried she could fall and hurt herself or an animal might kick her. Anything might happen.

"Come on, Sis," Tim said. "Have you found out what's involved and given thought to the possibility of Louise going?"

"To a birthday party? After what happened to her and her dad?"

"Sorry… I do see…You have to let her do some things though."

"You tell her she can do anything and sometimes she just can't."

"She can't walk, but that doesn't mean she can't ever achieve anything. Look at Franklin Roosevelt, Tanni Grey Thompson and Stephen Hawking."

Misha smiled. "She's not going to be president of the United States."

Tim grinned back. "OK, you got me there. Perhaps she won't be a famous scientist or athlete either, but we don't know that. Perhaps she'll be a librarian, secretary, work in a factory shoving things into boxes, become a teacher, check out girl or comedian. Point is, there are things she could try and I don't just mean for a job."

"I suppose." Tim was right. By trying to protect her daughter, Misha was adding to the restrictions Louise faced. She'd been so excited by the idea of a birthday party and even more by seeing all the farm animals. Misha had hated saying no, but she'd done it without considering the alternative.

"OK you can take her to the New Forest this weekend. Try to keep her hopes a bit realistic though?"

"I'll think about it." He winked as he said it. "And while we're thinking about things, Gordon is probably free this weekend."

It wasn't just Louise who rarely went out. Misha was no more willing to risk hurt for herself than she was for her daughter. Tim's friend Gordon had asked her out several times. She couldn't make her brother understand why she continued to refuse, despite liking him.

"Louise gets on well with him and you know I'd be more than happy to babysit."

"I know." She also knew that to accept a date was to allow in hopes, perhaps even expectations, and they'd just get crushed again.

Tim pecked her cheek. "Gotta go. I'll see you tomorrow."

As Louise waited for her uncle to collect her, she chattered excitedly about unicorns.

"Louise, love, I don't think you're very likely to see any," Misha warned.

"Of course not, Mummy. They're very, very rare. Hardly anyone ever sees one."

Maybe Tim was doing his best to be realistic after all. If he was sticking to his promise, maybe she should too. She'd told Louise she'd think about the party invitation and as Tim had pointed out, she hadn't actually done so.

Once Tim and Louise left, Misha rang the birthday girl's mother. "I'm sorry to be a pain, but if it's not too late, could you give me a few more details?"

"Of course." The woman explained that the farm they were visiting often hosted children's parties. The various animals could all be reached from smooth concrete paths, easily wide enough for Louise's chair. She'd be able to stroke and feed them, even try milking the goat.

"The ponies are really quiet. You could lift Louise onto one's back and it'd just stand there or they could get it to walk really slowly. If not, there's a little cart one of them pulls and there's a wheelchair ramp to get her in. She could be driven round like a princess in a fairytale carriage."

"She'd love that," Misha admitted.

"Look, I know how scary it can be letting them go somewhere new. My eldest is allergic to nuts and I'm terrified his friends' mums will forget and feed him something he shouldn't eat. You're very welcome to come

125

and see she's OK. Do you want to think it over and let me know in a day or so?"

"Thank you. Yes, I'll do that."

She did. Instead of imagining herself waiting at home, terrified a phone call or knock at the door was about to bring bad news, she thought about Louise enjoying herself with her friends and Misha being right there with her.

Tim had been right. She'd given the idea so little thought it hadn't even occurred to her that she could go too. Louise would receive other invitations, wouldn't she? Next time, when it was just for tea not a party, Misha would really think before giving her answer. She'd seriously consider saying yes.

She'd also make a lot more effort to have Louise's friends come and visit her. No more vague promises followed by excuses. Misha checked her diary for possible dates and made a list of suitable films for Louise to choose from.

Louise was bubbling over with excitement when Tim brought her home.

"We saw one. Mummy! We saw a unicorn! Uncle Tim said it was just an ordinary pony but it wasn't. It was a unicorn without a horn!"

Misha laughed. "How do you know?"

"It was different from all the others. Instead of running away it just stood still and looked at me. I could sort of feel it… like it was giving me a wish."

"We didn't go close," Tim assured her.

"No, we didn't. Uncle Tim said you can't catch a unicorn but I really wanted to stroke a pony and he didn't let me go near them either." Louise sighed.

"They're wild, sweetheart. It could be dangerous," Tim said.

"Uncle Tim is right, love. He was just looking after you. Now, who's going to explain the bits of grass sticking to your trousers?"

"We sat on the ground and had a picnic," Louise said.

"I see." And she did. Louise hadn't sat in her chair watching the fun. Tim had lifted her out so she could have a taste of it herself.

"Can you manage to change them yourself?"

"Yes, Mummy."

"It was just a few grapes and some carrot sticks," Tim said the moment she'd left the room.

Misha nodded. "It's OK and I'm sorry," she told her brother. "I see now you weren't giving her unrealistic hopes, just allowing her to have fun."

"Having fun is important, Sis. Um… the thing is…"

Misha spoke over him. "Before I change my mind or lose my nerve, are you free next Sunday afternoon?"

"Yes. Why?"

Misha pressed redial on her phone. "Hi. Louise would love to come to the party, but I'd like myself and my brother to be there so we can lift her and well…"

"That's no problem at all. We all know Tim from the school gate and he explained about Louise's accident. If there's anything else you need to know, or you've got any concerns, just give me a call."

"I'm sure it will be fine," Misha managed to say before she rang off.

"It will, won't it?" she asked her brother. "You'll help me get through this?"

He hugged her. "You're doing the right thing, Sis. You'll see that as soon as you tell Louise she can go."

"I expect you're right. Oh sorry, you started to say something?"

"Yes. Well, we bumped into my mate Gordon. It was a total accident honest and I didn't put her up to it, I swear."

"Put who up to what?"

"Louise told him that you never get to go out except for work and shopping and I might just have happened to mention you like Chinese food and..."

Misha's phone beeped to say she'd got a text.

"That's probably him, asking you to dinner."

Misha checked. "It is."

"What are you going to say?"

"I don't know. I'll have to think about it." She gave her brother a wink, before going to make Louise's happy mood even better.

22. New For Old

"Can you get the tree out the loft?" Julie asked her husband. She was busy making a list for the food they'd need on Christmas Day. Pancetta and celeriac were apparently vital ingredients for modern festive fair, along with filo pastry for herb butter parcels. They sounded classy, tasty – and fiddly to do. Still, if you wanted everything just right, you had to put in the effort.

"Alright," he said but didn't get up from his chair.

"Now, Stuart, or you'll forget."

"No, I…" he started to say.

Julie guessed he'd been going to deny it. Just as well he didn't or she'd remind him about the carpet offcuts, letter from the health centre and overgrown shrub by the front door, all of which he'd promised to do something about. No doubt he meant it when he said it, but then some distraction put it from his mind.

"It's too early to put up the tree yet," Stuart told her, changing tack.

He had a point, but then she wasn't ready to put it up just yet. She wanted to check the lights still worked and buy new baubles. This year's look seemed to be bright reds and citrus shades, judging by what she'd seen in the shops – both their displays and what they were offering for sale. They looked lovely – so fresh and vibrant. If Stuart had his way, the decorations would stay in the loft until Christmas Eve and they'd still be using the second-hand ones they'd had for their first Christmas.

"They're traditional," Stuart had claimed. "Isn't that what Christmas is about? Well, that and the obvious."

Julie's head was so full of the things she wanted to buy she didn't stop to consider how 'the obvious' fitted into her plans. "Partly, but also sparkle and style and fun. Besides if we've gone to the trouble and expense of having decorations, we might as well enjoy them for more than just a few days."

Eventually Julie got her way. The tree was brought down and assembled. Stuart tested the lights and had them strung up before she knew it, giving her no time to suggest they get different ones for a change. Before she'd even looked at the decorations, Stuart slid her gift under the tree.

Julie had a fairly shrewd idea what was inside: a handbag. She'd been dropping none too subtle hints about wanting a new one for quite some time.

'I hope it doesn't rain, or the books will be soaked by the time I get to the library. My poor old bag isn't waterproof any longer,' was one. 'I stopped off in the museum to look at the vintage clothing display. I kept my bag tucked inside my coat in case anyone thought I was walking off with an exhibit,' was another.

"Look how creased the leather is," she said one day, holding it up for him to see.

Stuart pointed to his face. "Know the feeling. You don't just get rid of a classic because you've had it a long time."

When he came to bed smelling of her moisturiser, she wondered if he'd jumped to the wrong conclusion about what she hoped to upgrade. However the next day he remarked on how many different styles of handbag there were.

"How do you know which is a good one?" he'd asked.

Immediately Julie regretted her plan to persuade him to buy one for her. If he did, she'd have to use it whatever it was like. She wouldn't want to hurt his feelings after he'd tried to please her and she couldn't very well say it didn't fit, could she? All Stuart knew about fashion was that flares no longer qualified as trendy. She was still working on getting him to give up tank tops.

Julie wanted a new bag, but not just any bag. It had to be the right one. Why hadn't she asked for vouchers? That way she could buy something she really liked and do so in the sales, so Stuart's money went a bit further. Maybe it wasn't too late? The reason she'd not yet replaced her handbag was that she'd not seen anything exactly right.

"It needs to be well made from durable materials," Julie told him. "And big enough to hold everything I need and I feel a classic design is best as it goes with everything."

Stuart had nodded at all that and Julie was relieved. Although not very modern in his outlook, Stuart did appreciate quality. He wouldn't buy her a garish, outdated knock-off from the market which would look tatty in next to no time.

That confidence evaporated when Stuart placed the wrapped box under the still undecorated tree.

"I'll make us a cup of tea," he said.

Julie barely heard him. The only type of handbag which would fit in there was one of those silly little clutch ones. Admittedly some of them looked very nice, but they were totally impractical for carrying more than cash and a door key. If you wanted to carry a lipstick, tissues, phone, bank cards, comb and pen you were out of luck. Julie needed those things and… her thoughts were interrupted by what sounded like a mug smashing onto the kitchen floor.

"Stuart?"

When no response came she went into the kitchen. She'd been right about the smashed mug. Stuart was staring at it and slurring something about his arm.

Julie grabbed the phone. "Ambulance please, I think my husband is having a stroke."

"He's lucky. It's just a mini stroke and as you called us so promptly he'll be fine," she was told a few hours later.

It didn't seem lucky to Julie until she came back the following day and, after walking through a ward of clearly very ill people, saw Stuart looking just as usual.

"My blood pressure was very high, but it's already coming down. I should be out tomorrow and if I follow the advice I've been given and take the medication they've prescribed, I'll be alright." When he joked it had just been a ploy to get out of doing the Christmas decorations she accepted that he really was going to be fine.

"OK, I'll do them but that means I get to have exactly what I want."

"Fair enough, love."

On trend glitz and glitter no longer seemed at all important. What she wanted was Stuart home and well. It didn't matter what the tree looked like, nor what was under it as long as she had him with her.

"I feel awful, nagging you to fetch everything down from the loft," she said. She was worried too about the stress of finding her gift.

"It's not your fault, love. I should have listened to you when you wanted me to go for that health check. I've learned my lesson and won't be so stubborn in future."

As Julie decorated the tree that afternoon she felt she too was learning a lesson. These last few years she'd paid more attention to the new decorations in the shops than the ones they'd had for years. How could she have dismissed as old-fashioned the delicate glass stars her mother had passed on to them for their first Christmas together? They were gorgeous and carried so many happy memories. So did the knitted donkey, sheep and camels Stuart's mother had made. The nativity could never be out of style at Christmas. Then there were the 'baby's first Christmas' baubles for each of their children and papier-mâché angels and Santas they'd made at school. Every item, except the straggly tinsel, was precious and beautiful in its own way.

Two weeks later Julie had the best Christmas present she could wish for; Stuart home and well and all their children with them. Thinking of Stuart's health, Julie had cooked up a turkey crown and plenty of healthy steamed vegetables. As they tucked into sprouts, carrots and red cabbage she realised she enjoyed the simple, traditional meal just as much as the imaginative alternatives she'd served up in the past.

The children approved too, saying it reminded them of when they were little.

"Best Christmas dinner you've cooked in years, love," Stuart said. "I hope I've done half as well in choosing your present." He handed her the box which had been sitting under the tree since before his stay in hospital.

Julie ripped off the paper, lifted the lid and tried to give a delighted smile. She felt it transform into a puzzled frown. Inside the box was a plastic 'bag for life'.

"It's what you said you wanted," Stuart said. He had trouble keeping a straight face as he continued, "Waterproof, strong and you can get lots in it. Classic design and… " He tapped the supermarket logo, "It's a well known brand."

When he and the children laughed, Julie joined in. There were times when she must be hard to please. She didn't blame Stuart for jokingly pointing that out. Probably he'd intended to get her another gift, but due to his health problems it had slipped his mind.

"I suppose you're right," Julie admitted. "I'd been looking for ages myself and couldn't find anything as nice or suitable as my old one."

"Bag or husband?" Stuart asked.

"Bag. Despite what I might say from time to time, I've never been tempted to replace you."

"Sometimes it's best to stick with what you know." From behind the sofa he produced another wrapped package.

Inside was a soft new replica of Julie's old bag.

"It's hand made," Stuart explained when she asked where he'd found it. "A classic and built to last. Just like me, I hope."

23. The Day British Time Stood Still

"Good job," the midwife said, as Mrs Duncansby-Smythe pushed her child into the world.

"It's a boy?" she asked.

"Yes, a big healthy boy."

As nurses attended her with hot towels and a fresh silk nightie, the new mother allowed herself to relax for a moment. Her purpose in life was almost complete – she just had the spare to produce in two or three year's time.

"Have you decided on a name?"

Mrs Duncansby-Smythe looked momentarily confused, but her frown soon cleared. Of course the midwife would be unaware which of her and her husbands relatives and connections was the most affluent and influential. "Giles."

"And will Daddy be here soon?"

"Daddy? No of course not... Oh, you mean my husband? Yes, quite soon. He's at a very important meeting." Awash with hormones and pethidine she decided to add her husband's name of Oscar to that of the child.

Giles Oscar Duncansby-Smythe's father missed other events in his son's life, but that was to be expected – he paid the bills and saw to it the child was never neglected. A nanny was always there, or one of the other staff. And the boy saw quite a lot of his mother of course. Mr Duncansby-Smythe enrolled Giles into the right schools.

He became a full boarder at seven. The headmaster reported, "a few issues settling".

"So did I," his father said. "Cried myself to sleep for weeks, but I've turned out just fine." That last was frequently disputed, but never in his hearing.

As intended, Giles's schooling introduced him to the people who'd ensured he got on in life. The billions he'd since acquired paid for all the therapy he needed, and the title he'd earned through favours done, gave him a feeling of self worth. He'd even had his share of love and loyalty from a succession of Red Setters the family bred for just that purpose. However not everyone was impressed.

A newspaper article on Sir Giles Duncansby-Smythe's achievements received letters, and comments on social media, saying it was easy for those born with silver spoons in their mouths. That all he'd succeeded in doing was to appoint staff who kept his father's entertainment empire afloat for the three decades he'd occupied the old man's office. That his greatest skill was to strategically lose at golf when playing those who'd keep his life out of the rough.

Sir Giles had nothing to prove. His critics were wrong. He was proud of himself and the work he did. His father must be proud too, as he'd not expressed disappointment for some time. It was true though that it wasn't Giles' name on the company stationery, that he'd not made something from nothing, not demonstrated his power. He could do all that.

Sir Giles Oscar Duncansby-Smythe founded GODS publishing. Not newspapers. He'd have enjoyed that level of easy power, but knew those who already had it wouldn't share. He published books. It was far harder to influence people that way, as people who read books had an infuriating tendency to think. There were compensations though. Pretty young novelists could often be persuaded to get between his sheets in order to see their name on a cover in a bookshop.

The publishing company thrived. ODS TV, one of his father's creations, promoted new releases with hyperbolic fervour on their morning shows, which helped. The TV company itself made a fortune from big name, big budget, drama series from any 'based on real events' stories containing enough slander or inaccuracies to be labelled controversial.

Diaries were Sir Giles's latest venture. One of his children, the oldest probably, had given him one as a gift. G.O.D-S. had been embossed in gold onto the smooth leather. He liked it so much he'd told his secretary to write in the names of each of his children on the anniversary of their births. Then he decided everyone should carry a memory of the great man – Giles.

"Great idea, sir," his advisors said in the meeting he'd scheduled to demonstrate his brilliance.

"But possibly a bit late for this year?" one idiot, called Caruthers, piped up.

"Oh, how so?" Sir Giles demanded.

The idiot cleared his throat a few times and stuttered through his explanation. "We couldn't have them in the shops until November and by then people will only be interested in buying stuff with red hearts on the packaging and chocolate eggs."

That got a few nods of agreement.

"You're exaggerating," Sir Giles said, which got more enthusiastic nods. Sir Giles wasn't prepared to be made a fool of in meetings, so he took the precaution of hacking into employees' computers to check what they were working on.

"I believe the point you're trying to make, Caruthers," he said in his most patronising tone, "is that sales would be low especially as we're a new name in this area, so a small print run would be advisable to avoid a large surplus of stock, and that smaller print runs are less profitable?"

"Precisely, sir."

"And you thought that wouldn't have occurred to me?"

"Well… I, that is…"

"Diaries are fairly standard things. Same size, paper quality, number of pages and all that. Even the layout is pretty much identical. We just need to move either the numbers, or days of the week, along a place or two. That's very easily done with digital technology. We're going to do a massive run. One fifteenth will be for this year and the rest will be for the next five years."

"Excellent idea, sir," and other words to that effect, echoed round the room.

The idiotic Caruthers looked as though he was trying hard not to say something.

"Anyone see a problem with this plan?" Sir Giles dared them all.

Nobody admitted to it if they did.

"Well you should!" he bellowed. "Storage! But fortunately someone has a working brain round here. We're warehousing them in the Crow building."

"The one the… Some people… That is…"

"The one I've been coming under pressure to allow to be used as a homeless shelter because it's been empty so long? Precisely, Caruthers. Kill two birds with one stone. Now, anyone else want to waste my time, or are we done here?"

The 2022 diary, sold in 2021 at twice the price of any other on the market, was a hit. It was a well designed, quality item. However it was their scarcity which made them most desirable. Apparently you weren't anybody if Sir Giles wasn't telling you what day of the week it was. He'd overheard his father say so at the club and been so overcome with emotion he'd considered hugging the old man.

The 2023 version of the GODS diary, available at a considerably higher price, sold out before Hallowe'en 2022.

"Another print run, sir?" an advisor suggested.

"No," Sir Giles said. "Leave them wanting more." He was right, as the law of averages dictates a man who makes so many decisions must sometimes be.

It was late on Christmas Eve when Sir Giles was involved in a conversation in which the fact that 2024 was to be a leap year was mentioned. He realised immediately that the digital manipulation he'd employed to realign the diaries without stopping the print run wouldn't have allowed for that. He called Caruthers who agreed that was the case.

"Fetch me a copy," he demanded.

"Now?"

"Of course now."

"But, sir, it's Christmas Eve."

"Are you trying to be funny, Caruthers? Think I don't know the date and need to check? You've been drinking I suppose."

Caruthers wisely avoided responding to the first part of the outburst. As he'd sipped a small glass of mulled wine at the carol concert in which his children, Tara and Peter, had performed he admitted to consuming alcohol. He'd be in the wrong regardless and it might get him out of a late night drive across the city.

"I'll send my driver over," Sir Giles generously offered.

Locating a copy of the 2024 diary first involved locating the key holder and then someone who knew what was kept where in the cavernous storerooms of the Crow building. The whole task took over two hours.

"This will cost me," Sir Giles roared, brandishing the offending diary.

"Not really, sir. The economies of scale mean you'll still be significantly in profit overall."

He might have got away with that, but for once Sir Giles wasn't thinking in purely financial terms.

"Someone's monumental incompetence will make me look a fool."

Perhaps a heavy dose of sycophantic pandering could have soothed him, but Caruthers didn't have the stomach for more than a token effort. Worse, he attempted to relieve his nausea with the truth.

"A mistake was made, but it's all of your own doing. I attempted to warn you of this precise situation in the initial meeting, but your bullying management style made it impossible."

"I'm neither wrong, nor a bully and as you clearly don't have the intelligence to realise that, your employment is terminated immediately."

Caruthers went home to place filled stockings at the foot of Tara and Peter's beds, and then to dream of working short enough hours to spend time with them, and to do so for an employer who didn't hold him in contempt.

Sir Giles didn't dream. He schemed. As his wife, various offspring, and their progeny, unwrapped the gifts Sir Giles' had told someone to order for them, he had someone else wrap the 2024 diary. It was delivered to No. 10 Downing Street along with a note stating, 'Our great nation's future' and bearing Sir Giles's flamboyant signature.

"What's this all about, Piles?" The PM asked at their club a few days later.

For a long time that hated nickname, coined in the school dormitory, had been consigned to history. Sir Giles did his best not to notice that the election result had brought about its return. "Turn to the end of February," he advised.

The PM did so, then consulted his Chinese made smartphone. "Bit of a blunder there old boy."

"No, a glorious opportunity." Sir Giles permitted himself a satisfied smile. "We're currently dictated to by the whole world on one issue or another and it's not good enough. Time to make a stand. Scrap the leap year. It will be your legacy."

"Won't it make business difficult? We'll be on different dates to everyone else."

"Not just different, we'll be ahead!"

"Ye-es."

"We're in a different time zones to everyone else, this is just an extension of that."

Seeing that the sheer force of his enthusiasm was not producing the blind obedience he'd come to expect, Sir Giles changed tack and tried his own dark brand of cajolery. He reminded the PM of an incident or two during their school days, and a few more during the PM's rise to his current position, and uttered the magical phrase 'legacy' several more times.

It nearly worked. In fact it would have done had it not been for the PM's affair just nine months before young Caruthers was born. He'd never publicly acknowledged the boy, but he'd occasionally done what he could for him, including getting him the job with Sir Giles's company.

Caruthers, at the request of his absent father, had gathered incriminating information on Sir Giles. Loyalty to his employer had prevented him passing it on, until his former boss became the defendant in his current lawsuit for wrongful dismissal.

The PM didn't want to scrap the leap year, and despite Sir Giles's thinly disguised blackmail, he didn't have to. Thanks to the efforts of his son and others, he had far more on Sir

Giles than the billionaire had on him. He did rather like the idea of a legacy though, a popular one that is. Sir Giles's talk of time zones had got him thinking. Switching the clocks twice a year from Greenwich Mean Time to British Summer Time was a faff. He'd scrap that and have the country permanently on Great British Time.

To give the public the illusion of choice, he held a referendum on whether to stick with GMT or BST. The issue divided families, almost brought down Facebook, and provided a smoke screen for scores of political moves. The votes, as always with these things, were split 48 to 52.

From then on the British public didn't ever change their clocks. They didn't change their PM either until he attempted to rescue a Golden Labrador from a canal two years later. Attempted, succeeded and subsequently drowned. The party, hoping this heroism would reflect well on them, called for a general election. His son is standing.

Caruthers didn't become a boarder until he was twelve, but he went to the right schools. There he met the people who could ensure he got on in life. He even has a dog, the offspring of one of Sir Giles' Red Setters, so he's sure to get in. He might even do a good job.

24. Just Say Yes

"No," Liz told her daughter. It was her fourth negative response during their phone chat, but as it was in response to, "Is there anything wrong?" it shouldn't count.

"You've been to the museum though? What's the latest exhibition?" Bella asked.

"I've no idea."

"Oh… What's new in the coffee shop? I can't get fatter just hearing about their fantastic puddings."

"You're not fat, love. Neither will I be as I don't go there now."

After the call Bella sent an internet link, 'To cheer you up'. Why? Had Liz said anything to cause worry?

Probably it was what she hadn't said. Bella was unlikely to be bothered her mother wasn't seeing much of Mike, but she might be concerned she wasn't going out or having fun, either alone or with another friend. Liz really was fine, but if she wanted to convince Bella of that she needed something better than reciting the TV schedule to say during their next conversation. What? It wasn't as though she was inundated with interesting opportunities.

She'd received invitations, but none she felt able to accept. Mike had been a good friend of her dear husband's. Of hers too throughout her long and happy marriage, but all that was in the past. In order to prevent the awkwardness of her repeated refusals when Mike suggested spending more time together, Liz now avoided places she used to enjoy visiting. It seemed sensible not to visit the museum where Mike volunteered. Prudent to keep away from the coffee shop where they'd fallen into the habit of meeting once or twice a week. Strangely, although Bella knew her mother had Mike's company at those places, she seemed to almost want Liz to keep going. Oh, of course she did – nobody likes to think of those they love sitting in front of the TV all day every day. Liz just needed to talk about something else and all would be well.

At least she could report having watched the video clip Bella sent. Liz chuckled at the footage of baby goats playing. They were so cute and very funny. Those leaps and twists off the hay bales were incredible. When the clip ended, Liz spotted links to other animal videos and enjoyed a few before noticing the phrase 'this clever hack is easiest ways to crochet button holes ever!' She always found button holes tricky, so clicked on that. Disappointingly the method was exactly what she did herself. Or used to. She hadn't crocheted anything for ages. The outings she'd taken with Mike, to galleries and gardens, had left little time for it and she'd not taken it up again.

Liz was about to log off when she saw someone who looked like her youngest granddaughter was documenting a 'say yes' challenge. The concept was simple – she'd say yes to absolutely everything unless it wasn't safe, legal or affordable. The girl agreed to everything from bungee jumping and wild swimming, to babysitting and litter picking.

"I feel so much more positive about everything now," she enthused. "I don't still say yes automatically, but neither do I immediately think only of the negative possibilities and say no to things if I'm not sure they're for me. Everyone should try this, even if it's just for the rest of the day. All you need do is start saying yes. Will you?"

"Yes," Liz surprised herself by saying.

Ten minutes later her neighbour called. "I'm going shopping, would you like anything?"

"Yes," Liz said. "Something to crochet."

"I don't know anything about wool, I'd get the wrong thing. I can drop you off on my way to the supermarket and pick you up if you like?"

"Yes please."

"I'll be an hour."

"Yes. I mean that's fine."

The expected browse at the craft shop didn't happen as the owner explained they were just about to close for refurbishment. "You can buy bags of assorted yarn at a bargain price and get a free pattern."

Liz bought everything she'd need for colourful tops for each of her granddaughters and then, because the owner said, "How about this?' and Liz was determined to say yes whenever she could, also bought the makings of a jazzy waistcoat.

Outside she was asked, "Can you spare some change?"

"Yes." She used the money to buy him a cup of soup.

There was time to kill, so when asked if she'd accept a free chocolate bar in exchange for answering a few marketing questions she said yes.

As she'd guessed, there were more than a few questions, but it was fascinating to see what went into promoting a new product. Of course Liz was asked about the taste and texture but there were questions about whether the name had any emotional impact on her, what she thought of the wrapper's colour, even the font of the words printed on it.

She was cold by the time she'd finished so she went into the coffee shop she'd avoided for the last fortnight.

Liz asked what the waitress recommended so she could say yes to the suggestions. As she waited for her warm ginger cake and cinnamon custard, which sounded perfect for the weather, she was aware of someone standing quite close.

She looked up. Mike!

The man who, other than her late husband, had been her closest friend for decades. Right until she realised they were dangerously close to becoming more. She'd been shocked by feelings she'd never thought to experience again and panicked. She'd refused every time he suggested doing something together and stopped going to places where she might bump into him. That had been a mistake.

"May I join you?" he asked.

If she accepted she risked... Happiness. That and having plenty to talk about with Bella! "Yes."

Thank you for reading this book. I hope you enjoyed it. If you did, I'd really appreciate it if you could leave a short review on Amazon and/or Goodreads.

To learn more about my writing life, hear about new releases and get a free short story, sign up to my newsletter – https://mailchi.mp/677f65e1ee8f/sign-up or you can find the link on my website patsycollins.uk

More Books by Patsy Collins

Novels

Firestarter
Escape To The Country
A Year And A Day
Paint Me A Picture
Leave Nothing But Footprints
Acting Like A Killer

Non-fiction –

From Story Idea To Reader
(co-written with Rosemary J. Kind)

A Year Of Ideas:
365 sets of writing prompts and exercises

Short story collections –

Just A Job
Perfect Timing
A Way With Words
Dressed To Impress
Coffee & Cake
Not A Drop To Drink
Criminal Intent
Making A Move

Over The Garden Fence
Up The Garden Path
Through The Garden Gate
In The Garden Air
Beyond The Garden Wall

No Family Secrets
Can't Choose Your Family
Keep It In The Family
Family Feeling
Happy Families

All That Love Stuff
With Love And Kisses
Lots Of Love
Love Is The Answer

Slightly Spooky Stories I
Slightly Spooky Stories II
Slightly Spooky Stories III
Slightly Spooky Stories IV